LOVECRAFT

LOVECRAFT
A STUDY IN
THE FANTASTIC

MAURICE LÉVY
Translated by S. T. Joshi

WAYNE STATE UNIVERSITY PRESS   DETROIT   1988

Library of Congress Cataloging-in-Publication Data
Lévy, Maurice.
   [Lovecraft. English]
   Lovecraft, a study in the fantastic / Maurice Lévy; translated by S. T. Joshi.
      p. cm.
   Translation of: Lovecraft, ou, Du fantastique.
   Revision of the author's thesis (Ph.D.)—Sorbonne, 1969.
   Bibliography: p.
   Includes index.
   ISBN 0-8143-1955-6 (alk. paper).   ISBN 0-8143-1956-4 (pbk.: alk. paper)
   1. Lovecraft, H. P. (Howard Phillips), 1890-1937—Criticism and interpretation.   2. Fantastic fiction, American—History and criticism.   3. Psychoanalysis and literature.   I. Title.
PS3523.0833Z7313 1988
813'.52—dc19   87-36470
                                                                    CIP

CONTENTS

Translator's Preface 7

Author's Preface 9

Introduction 11

1. The Outsider   17

2. Dwellings and Landscapes   35

3. The Metamorphoses of Space   45

4. The Horrific Bestiary   55

5. The Depths of Horror   63

6. The Horrors of Heredity   73

7. Cthulhu   79

8. Unholy Cults   87

9. In the Chasms of Dream   97

10. From Fable to Myth   109

Conclusion 117

Abbreviations 121

Notes 123

Bibliography 135

Index 143

TRANSLATOR'S PREFACE

I should like to explain some curiosities in this translation. Professor Lévy's work was originally a doctoral dissertation (Sorbonne, 1969), full to the brim with footnotes and references. When, however, it was published in book form in 1972, two significant changes were made: first, all the footnotes were omitted; second (and much more important), Lévy extensively revised the whole text, dropping a few portions and adding a great many. It is unquestionable that this revision has radically improved the work; I have, therefore, translated directly from the book, although restoring some of the footnotes (adding a few of my own) and even inserting into the text a few portions of the original dissertation that had been omitted. I did not feel it necessary to reproduce all the footnotes from the dissertation, because many consisted only of quotations in English from Lovecraft's work, which English-speaking readers may be expected to know. My footnotes are enclosed in brackets. In some instances I have altered Professor

Lévy's footnotes (to indicate some recent publication of an obscure work, for example); these footnotes bear both our initials.

I have also taken the liberty of making corrections in some passages of the book, particularly Lévy's discussion of Lovecraft's myth-cycle (chapter 7). Lévy was, in 1972, working from seriously erroneous views about the myth-cycle propagated by August Derleth, and the combined work of such scholars as Dirk W. Mosig, Richard L. Tierney, Robert M. Price, and David E. Schultz has cleared away the Derlethian encrustations. My work has involved not so much rewriting as merely omitting passages that are now demonstrably wrong. This is one of the few instances where Lévy's book has become "dated"; in every other particular his work is still breathtakingly ahead of its time.

The bibliography is largely of my own doing. Lévy's bibliography contained (aside from commonly known English publications by or about Lovecraft) a chronology of Lovecraft's fiction which—unbeknown to him or anyone else at the time—is not by Lovecraft but by August Derleth and therefore contains many errors; I have replaced it by a chronology that I have established and that has been accepted by other scholars. I have also added a fuller primary and secondary bibliography, including publications subsequent to Levy's work, and an index. Quotations of Lovecraft's work in the text derive from my recent corrected editions. References to books and articles in the notes are highly abridged; fuller information can be found in the list of abbreviations and the secondary bibliography.

It is now my happy task to thank the colleagues who have so kindly helped me in this translation. Foremost my thanks go to Professor Maurice Lévy, who not only examined and corrected this entire translation but with whom I spent some very pleasant hours discussing Lovecraft and other subjects when, by pure accident, he came to Providence, Rhode Island, when I was there in the fall of 1977. Dirk W. Mosig was my constant guide in Lovecraft studies, and to him I owe more than can possibly be stated in so brief a space as this. Marc A. Michaud, Kennett Neily, Kenneth W. Faig, Donald R. Burleson, David E. Schultz, William Fulwiler, Robert M. Price, Will Murray, and others have also stimulated me. Sincere thanks also go to Professor Richard Blakely of Brown University, who extensively revised a portion of this manuscript and encouraged me to complete it. Last-minute suggestions by Robert M. Price and Thomas Ligotti have helped me significantly.

AUTHOR'S PREFACE

This little book is a dissertation that has been revised, lightened, and divested of its cumbrous critical apparatus.[1] My thanks go to Roger Asselineau, professor at the Sorbonne, who agreed to supervise it; to Jacques Cabau and Hélène Tuzet, whose stimulating remarks alerted me to many problems; to the directors of the John Hay Library in Providence, who permitted me to consult the rich collection of Lovecraftiana in their custody; to August Derleth, who regularly kept me posted on his new publications and sent them to me; to Frank Belknap Long, the "Sonny" of Lovecraft's letters, who evoked for me, in the course of long summer evenings in New York, the shade of his "Grandpa Theobald"; and to my cat Elmar, who told me of Ulthar.

INTRODUCTION

The object of this study is limited. Our goal is not to give the "case" of Howard Phillips Lovecraft[1] an exhaustive analysis; his personality is too rich, too complex for that. Moreover, the documents indispensable for properly carrying out such an undertaking are not all available. Although the two volumes of letters published to date, of the four (or five) promised by August Derleth,[2] permit us to hazard some ideas on the dreamer from Providence, large areas of his life are still left in darkness. His biography has yet to be written; perhaps one day it will come out.[3]

Nor is it a matter of proposing in these pages a prescriptive definition—one which would be the fruit of theoretical speculation—of the fantastic; others, better qualified than we, are working on this difficult task.[4] What we modestly wish to do is to add to the thick file of this literary genre an exemplary work and to draw from it some conclusions, which must be taken for what they are. Without in the least wishing to be dogmatic, we believe that these conclusions nevertheless are a result of an *oriented* reading of Lovecraft's tales. It will be left to the reader to decide if they in any way clarify this strange oeuvre, and if they can or cannot be applied to other authors.

This universe into which we are about to enter, with its bizarre dimensions and hideous monsters, where time and space stretch or contract in incomprehensible ways, merits analysis for more than one reason. It is a fantastic universe because of the manifestly dreamlike quality of the images that it presents and that compose it and because of the author's obvious intention to capture and to communicate his anguish. Let us admit that he succeeds admirably in so doing: his archaic horrors shake us, jar us from our certitudes, remove us for all too short a time from the soothing influence of the modern world. He leaves far behind him the comforts of the American dream, the reassuring slogans, the "Colgate smile," and explores the unsoundable depths of dream, carrying us along after him. Few authors went as far as he in depicting foulness; we know of none who have given to their work a structure analogous to the Cthulhu Mythos.[5]

Lovecraft does not yet hold, however, the place he deserves in the Pantheon of Horror. In the United States his only audience during his lifetime was that of the cheap magazines and journals that might be bought in a train station. After Lovecraft's death, August Derleth—himself a *fantaisiste* and poet—busied himself in finding other readers for Lovecraft. Derleth, since 1939, has published Lovecraft's tales in a form more worthy of his art; but what, in his country, is the effect of books issued in an edition of only three thousand copies?[6]

In France, Jacques Bergier and Louis Pauwels discovered and launched him. They had spoken of him as early as *Le Matin des magiciens*, and gave him a significant role in their great enterprise by publishing a tale of his in the first issue of *Planète*.[7] To them we owe our first encounter with the "grand génie venu d'ailleurs,"[8] and we are deeply grateful to them. Thanks to them, Lovecraft is, paradoxically, better known and more appreciated in France than in his own country. Whereas in the United States his former friends or correspondents are content largely with recalling memories—saying how he was sensitive to cold or fond of ice cream—[9] such articles as Claude Ernoult's in *Les Lettres Nouvelles* or Michel Deutsch's in *Esprit* place his art in its true position. The recent *Cahier de L'Herne* that was devoted to him not only made available the better American studies, but also stressed the Cthulhu Mythos, which gives Lovecraft's fantastic universe its full dimension.[10] Without wishing to make Lovecraft the "mythographer" of the twentieth century, the "rhapsodist" of modern times, we believe that this approach is the most accurate and fruitful.

The fantastic tradition is not, in the country of Edgar Allan Poe, as rich as one might believe it to be. Long after their political independence, the former colonies remained under the literary domination of Old England. The catalogues of the "circulating libraries" of the period[11] show conclusively that the "horrors" feeding the young nation were English in origin. The Gothic novels of Ann Radcliffe, M. G. Lewis, Regina Maria Roche, Francis Lathom, and many other less famous authors published by the Minerva Press scattered terror to every region, among the dairymaids and peasant laborers of New England[12] as well as among the ladies of the world.[13] And did not Thomas Jefferson himself, president of the United States, subscribe to the American edition of one of the most terrifying novels of the genre, William Henry Ireland's *The Abbess*?[14] One would think that it was to protest against the chimeras of another age that Charles Brockden Brown wrote *Edgar Huntly*[15] and most of his other novels. But his efforts to instill the strange into local folklore remained largely ineffectual, and we cannot conclude that he is a real precursor of American fantastic literature.

It is reasonable to mark the debut of the genre in the United States with Poe. Even here there is reason to add nuances and to qualify some standard affirmations in this field: Although it may be indisputable that "The Fall of the House of Usher" is a masterwork of the genre, there is yet in many of his tales only the macabre, the "arabesque," and the "grotesque."... By no means is the fantastic only that. Furthermore, "ratiocination"—essential in fantastic writing, corresponding to what we would today call the "function of rationality"—is in his work too clearly dissociated from the irrational. There is in Poe a dream side and a cerebral side, for example, "Metzengerstein" and "The Purloined Letter." These two stories are indeed "extraordinary tales," but in very different ways. To our mind, the fantastic is born from the divorce produced between the perfect lucidity of the characters and the dream-images that they encounter. Lacking any more precise criteria, one could almost measure the fantastic by the *degree of consciousness* of the heroes on one side, and on the other the *intensity of the dream-images* that surround them. Examined from this angle, only some tales fully deserve to be classified as fantastic. Yet what tales!—clearly the best written to this day.

There are, if not several kinds of fantasy, at least several methods of transcribing, through dramatization, the anguish at the source of all fantastic creation. The tales of Nathaniel Hawthorne are very different from those of Poe: Less dreamlike, more directly placed under the control of the intellect, they are distinguished above all by the importance accorded to fable, which is dense, articulated, and precise, rooted not in the lone phantasms of an individual psyche but in the past of an ethnic and religious community. These specters are discreet, immaterial, and faraway, really more allegorical than truly fantastic. And Hawthorne was able to give the "problem of problems," that of Evil, a supernatural dimension. Hawthorne had a sense of the mystery attached to dwellings; he knew what evil spells were affixed to those old houses in Salem, with their many gables and their facades blackened by the accumulated horrors of the past. But Hawthorne has anticipated still more directly the major theme of Lovecraft's tales in his depicting the diffuse and enveloping presence of the invisible. The characters, all perfectly conforming to the norm, move in a universe that one vaguely discerns as surpassing the limits of the verbal and the visible, a universe that has a *historical profundity,* rooted in the numinous.

Ambrose Bierce is more specifically fantastic insofar as his art, less subtle, less shaded, is the expression of an acerbic lucidity that borders on cynicism. One is almost tempted to believe that one day he decided to instill fear into his contemporaries *by hatred,* to gain revenge on them. To do this, he uses an aggressive, ferocious humor. The title of the first chapter of "The Damned Thing" is "One Does Not Always Eat What Is on the Table"; it concerns a cadaver placed there for an autopsy. The third chapter of the same tale is titled "A Man Though Naked May Be in Rags"; the man in question is dead. . . . Bierce has a sense of the concise, the secret formula for producing shock. We need only read his *Devil's Dictionary*[16] to be persuaded of this. Served by his style, he gives to his evil entities a density, a "thickness," which the evanescent chimeras of Hawthorne do not have. In "The Death of Halpin Frayser" and "The Middle Toe of the Right Foot" there are some spectacularly diabolical, cruel, and inimical presences. And "The Suitable Surroundings" shows the importance even he attached to the architectural framework of a tale that not only favors, but somehow evokes and even *creates* a fantastic event.

It is surely ridiculous to want to make Henry James a writer of fantasy in the full and exclusive sense of the term. There is in him, however, a somber vein, some nocturnal aspect, which in *The Turn of the Screw* finds a troubled expression. The ambiguity of the tale, the doubt that is sustained to the end as to the exact nature of the reported facts, which are suggested rather than described, attests to the high quality of his art. There is in his writing an aristocratic reserve, which, far from compromising his manifest purpose of disturbing, gives to the diabolism of his characters a more chilling relief. And that great staircase in the mansion, around which the evil of the tale materializes in spiral form, orients the dream toward unspeakable depths.[17]

Francis Marion Crawford not only wrote historical novels: There is vampirism in "For the Blood Is the Life," an old house and some apparitions in "The Dead Smile," and a nightmarish "presence" that incites the occupants of a ship's cabin to suicide in "The Upper Berth."[18] This author falls into the class of novelists who, on occasion, do not disdain from giving way to demons within the confines of a novelette. In this group we must also place Robert W. Chambers, whose *The King in Yellow*[19] contains several lovely pages of terror, and Mary E. Wilkins-Freeman, who, in *The Wind in the Rose-Bush*,[20] abandons the psychological realism and local color of her other tales to explore frighteningly forbidden realms.

We must agree on this: the American fantastic tradition lacks unity and depth. The reason for this is, perhaps, that it is not rooted, as in England, in a homogeneous and largely secular culture. It is important, however, to establish that the best writers here cited—with the possible exception of Hawthorne (but is he truly representative of the genre of fantasy?)—were certainly oriented toward Europe. What is there particularly American about Poe, fed completely as he was on the novels of the English "school of frenzy," and whose best tales develop themes as old as those of "mother Radcliffe"? Or about James, who was so English at heart? To create an adequate atmosphere for a fantastic tale, we must have old houses and medieval castles that materialize in space the hallucinatory presence of the past, the houses we can find *authentically* only on the old continent. We need an old, legendary foundation, a national heritage of obscure beliefs and antiquated super-

stitions. We need millennia of history, the progressive ac-
cumulation in the racial memory of prodigious facts and innumerable crimes, so that the necessary sublimations and schematizations
can take place. Above all, we need a history that has become myth,
so that the fantastic can be born through the irruption of myth into
history.

It was precisely Lovecraft's merit to discover, beyond the historical data of his own country, the structure of the great myths that
have nourished humanity. In *dreaming* the past of New England,
this home of sorcerers, he recommenced an archaic tradition, tran-
scending local peculiarities. The strange, the disquieting, the abnormal emerge from this surfacing of the primordial into the contemporary. America, too, can become a fantastic world, because it
was from Salem that Lovecraft re-created the Cosmos.

16

1
THE OUTSIDER

The aeons and the worlds are my sport, and I watch with calm and amused aloofness the anticks of planets and the mutations of universes.

—Lovecraft[1]

Lovecraft's friends have often asserted that the life and character of the "old gentleman of Providence," of "Grandpa Theobald" as he liked to call himself, was even more rich, even more fascinating, even more *fantastic* than his work. Judging by his letters—those innumerable and interminable epistles full of dream and humor, full of hate and despair—we can accept this verdict without much disagreement. Strange are the tales of H. P. Lovecraft, where monstrous "entities" and infamous deities share the Cosmos beyond the gulfs of time. But even stranger, even more disconcerting, was in many respects the existence led by this great loner, this pitiable paranoiac, the plaything of cosmic forces, who was compelled by

17

Yog-Sothoth, Nyarlathotep, and Cthulhu, whether by indifference, error, or malice, to live in an era in which he manifestly had no business.

Born in 1890, in that New England where the glory of the past haunts the present with such ceaseless insistence, he remained all his short life more familiar with his beloved eighteenth century, the era when Providence was still His Majesty's colony, than with the industrial era in which America was, not without its crises, engaged. In the autobiographical accounts that he frequently sent to his many correspondents, he stresses the unmixed purity of his lineal ancestry.[2] As much on the paternal side as the maternal, he had eyes only for the English immigrants: the Lovecrafts, coming from Devonshire in the early part of the nineteenth century; the Phillipses, orginating in Lincolnshire and established in New England since the end of the seventeenth century. To tell the truth, the details and the dates change from one letter to another, and we soon understand that these genealogical constructions are ever so little unreal—less fantastic, of course, than when he discovered a distant relationship with Machen,[3] but already permeated by dream. It is important to emphasize this pronounced taste for the familial past, this respect for the *line,* this mythical quest for origins; many are the characters in his tales who thus go off to search for themselves and who encounter the most dreadful adventures in their path. Horror is hidden in the most archaic layers of racial memory.

According to Lovecraft, there were among his ancestors only pastors, industrialists, and worthies. He who lived in misery liked to imagine the comfort that he knew as a child in the great and beautiful mansion of his maternal grandfather. All his life he would be haunted by the memory of this rich and cultivated man, who had traveled widely and who sketched for him the ruins of Pompeii. Conversely, he spoke little of his father, doubtless because he had hardly known him, but also perhaps because the circumstances of his death showed him—more than Lovecraft dared admit—for what he was. He said in a letter that his father was seized with paralysis in 1893, following an intense nervous breakdown, and that he passed the last five years of his life in a hospital, unconscious.[4] He was a paretic. Did Lovecraft ever know this? It is difficult to say, but the heavy ambiguities remain, in his remarks and . . . his silences.

His father dead, Lovecraft returned to live with the Phillipses, abusively cherished by a neurotic and possessive mother who was perhaps disturbed still more deeply by her knowledge of the nature of her husband's illness. There Lovecraft passed the happiest years of his life—in the house where he was born, where everything was familiar to him, where he had his roots. Later, exiled in New York among hordes of strangers, these images of his "native home" and his sheltered childhood were his only means of defense against madness and suicide. To his inmost self, Providence remained a haven, a place of rest, a dream city to which he could flee from alienating reality.

It was a solitary childhood, passed in the company of adults and old people, far from the games of boys of his own age. He was sent to school, but his poor health impelled long absences. He made up for these lost academic hours by abundant readings made at random from the rich family library. Very precocious, even brilliant, he was at an early age seized with a passion for Grimm, Poe, and Hawthorne, whose work he devoured. He was also fascinated by Greco-Roman mythology, which awakened his imagination: At an age when others were playing with hoops, he built altars where he offered divers sacrifices to Pan, Apollo, and Minerva.[5] At age eight he became interested in the sciences; a small chemical laboratory was installed for him in the basement,[6] where he made strange experiments. At age twelve he owned a small telescope and began scrutinizing the sky, the constellations of which he already knew. This attraction for the faraway worlds and unsoundable gulfs of the Cosmos eclipsed for a time all his other interests. He edited a paper, the *Rhode Island Journal of Astronomy*, entirely written by hand.[7] At age sixteen he knew enough about astronomy to publish articles on the sky and the stars in several Providence papers.[8]

His gifts isolated him still further from the world, gave him an awareness of his superiority, enveloped him in an aloofness not commensurate with his age. At school, when he went there, his classmates gave him little sympathy. "Thus repelled by humans," he wrote, "I sought refuge and companionship in books."[9]

At age eighteen his persisting ill-health, which was of obscure origins—he suffered from migraines, insomnia, and "nervous troubles"—did not permit him to enter Brown University. Despite his brilliant intelligence and wide culture, he remained incapable of regular, sustained effort. Thus he continued to read and work at his own pace, in a closed world where two aunts had, along with his mother, replaced the departed grandfather.

Precocious in literature as well as in science, he had begun to write; the tales were puerile, but already showed the themes that would obsess him all his life and would condition his artistic creation. In "The Beast in the Cave" (1905) and "The Alchemist" (1908) there are images of underground labyrinths, monsters, and disturbed heredity, which, in this "old adolescent," betray precocious fears, agonies that would long continue to haunt his dreams, and whose projection in the space and time of fiction perhaps took the form of an unconscious search for a therapeutic, the instinctive action of a sick man in search of a cure: He still wrote only for himself.

A chance now came, however, to open himself up to the world. The method was modest if we think of the activities of a boy of his age, but it was one that allowed this solitary recluse to express himself, almost to bloom. In 1914—he was twenty-four years old—he discovered the United Amateur Press Association, an organization composed of amateur writers who communicated their work by correspondence.[10] Lovecraft thus entered into epistolary contact with a variety of people, very different from himself in their tastes and activities, and over whom he quickly gained supremacy thanks to his undoubted talents. His first correspondents, Maurice W. Moe, Rheinhart Kleiner, and Ira A. Cole, formed the Kleicomolo, where each syllable was part of the name of the four participants.[11] Later Alfred Galpin joined them, forming, on the same principle, the Gallomo; and there were still others who, without entering into a definite circuit, began corresponding with him—Clark Ashton Smith, James F. Morton, and especially Frank Belknap Long, for whom Lovecraft always had a special predilection.

Thus, surrounded at a distance by invisible admirers, at the center of a tight network of complicated epistolary ties, Lovecraft could finally show his full ability: he had found his audience. "Dagon" (1917), "The Tomb" (1917), "Polaris" (1918), "The White Ship" (1919), and many other tales were first submitted to the criticism of this circle of educated amateurs.[12] The voluminous correspondence that was roused in return by each submission of Lovecraft's and the letters that he circulated to respond to the compliments or objections addressed to him[13] reveal a feverish activity, more than enough, it seems, to make him forget that such an existence, now that Europe was ravaged by war, was strange in the America of the twentieth century.

Of material cares he had none; his mother and his aunts were there to take care of them. Nor had he a professional occupation that would cut into his spare time. Lovecraft entered into adulthood with the same nonchalant independence, the same puerile carefreeness of his younger years, but also haunted by the same profound agonies, to which he would with time give a more and more artistic expression.

During these years Lovecraft lived, as he did all his life, with *indirect* human contacts. After the war he was elected president of the United,[14] and he henceforth devoted to it all his time and energies—especially when, after the death of his mother in the spring of 1921, he felt, suddenly and tragically, how frail was the edifice on which his life rested. In the same way as his native home, his mother had been for him a symbol of security and peace, even during the last two years, which she had spent in a psychiatric hospital. His equilibrium threatened, he readjusted to the world by new compensations and took refuge yet more deeply in dream, shifting the responsibility of his daily life to his aunts. His nightmares became blacker, his tales—"The Outsider" (1921), "Herbert West—Reanimator" (1921–22), "The Hound" (1922)— became more nocturnal. His prodigious egocentrism helped, however, to surmount his crisis. His physical health improved and, as much as his now dwindled finances permitted, he traveled. He went on humble antiquarian expeditions to Salem, Marblehead, Boston, and Portsmouth. There is a profound joy in the letters in which he speaks of the places he has visited. We sense that he is physically attached to these landscapes, to this earth. There his past is buried; there his destiny will play itself out. To New England, which was his birthplace and which he thus discovered by stages, he was intimately and absolutely tied.

Now past the age of thirty, he, as always, was without a profession. Had his mother not eternally protected him against all excess fatigue? Had she not convinced him, by constantly taking his place, that he was inept in the affairs of the world? And what need was there for a professional dreamer to find a stable job? Since youth he had thrown himself into the work of revision by correspondence, where he could at least exercise his epistolary talents, and where his schedule was only a little constraining. The checks for a few dollars—irregular and widely spaced—that he received in return, with a meager income from the scattered remnants of the family inheritance, were enough for his needs.

Into this sheltered life there suddenly appeared an ordeal. At a meeting of the United Amateur Press Association held in Boston in 1921, Lovecraft met one of his revision clients, Mrs. Sonia Greene of Brooklyn—of Russian Jewish origin, widowed, and about ten years his elder. Despite his racial prejudices, he was enticed by her charm, her grasp of reality, her kindness. Could this business-woman who so competently managed a store on Fifth Avenue perhaps take his destiny in her hands and replace his departed mother? He married in March 1924 and settled with her in New York.

It is hard to imagine a couple more ill-matched: he, spineless, lost in bizarre dreams, preoccupied solely with chimeras; she, active, energetic, above all concerned with the future. And yet, the first weeks were happy. Lovecraft discovered New York, with its museums and its libraries, and met again his correspondents—Kleiner, Morton, Long—with whom he took long nocturnal walks. He who previously had had eyes only for the old towns of the past now admired the Marvelous City from Manhattan Bridge in all its fiery brilliance at twilight.[15]

But in New York one could not live like an aesthete for long; one must think of work. Then came the time of humiliation, of adver-tisements in the newspapers, of interviews where his sickly tim-idity, his *gaucherie*, put him at a disadvantage. Disenchantment and bitterness followed his puerile initial enthusiasm. He was no longer looking at New York at a distance; he lived there, in all its filth and promiscuity. The times of sublimations were gone. He, the pure-blooded Viking, brushed daily in the street against strangers with repulsive faces, the sight or contact of whom dis-gusted him.

Soon his wife left him, to take a more remunerative position in Cleveland. Such was, at any rate, the reason given. What had really passed between them? Nothing, surely, too dramatic: Love-craft was too chivalrous to arouse any estrangement. But he was too egotistical, too listless to make a suitable husband. Was he, moreover, perhaps incapable of fully assuming the role?[16] In any case, he was now alone, in a city he now loathed, far from all that was of value to him, unable to find a job, and unable to decide whether to return to Providence. He could not make a decision. He hid his misery in the slums of Brooklyn, had ten-cent dinners, and lost forty pounds in a few months.

He now saw his friends only intermittently, ashamed of his threadbare clothes. He spent his days wandering futilely in search of employment, or sitting on a park bench. The nights he spent in writing. We must read "He" (1925) and "The Horror at Red Hook" (1925) to fathom the depths of his despair. In this artificial city, he says, this lonely hybrid place removed from the great currents of civilization, in this "kennel of feverish mongrels,"[17] he felt himself a rootless stranger. Under a false playfulness, the hatred and despair pierce through his letters. But what doubtless hurt him most was to be left to himself. He who was so brilliant in his work was a failure in life. Somebody had to look out for his health and safety, else he would plunge into the abyss. Who knows what would have come to pass had it not been for the friendship of Frank Belknap Long? The young disciple wrote to one of Lovecraft's aunts, who still lived in Providence, and the invitation that he had so hoped for, so waited for, but which he never had the courage to ask for himself, came. In the spring of 1926, after two years spent in hell, he finally regained heaven. Or rather, this ecstatic return to his native land was in effect a return to the maternal breast. There is something moving in the account he gives of this mythical return to his home, something that betrays a vital, primordial experience.

Soon he had settled down again, on College Hill, in his usual habits and his dreams. Again there was a feminine presence watching over him, discrete, competent, and *nonconjugal*. Again there was raised around him that familiar landscape of roofs, domes, and steeples he had known and loved as a child. He shook off the dust from his clothes, threw the bitter images of New York into the outer darkness, and—in this ancient city where his personal history coincided with the past—rediscovered his identity.

In this beatific setting, in the very places of his childhood, he spent the ten or so years he had left to live. He wrote unstintingly, not only for a limited circle of friends but now for a larger public, that of the magazines specializing in horror: *Astounding Stories, Marvel Tales, Home Brew,*[18] and above all *Weird Tales,* from the time of its founding in 1923. He complained of the primitive tastes of his readers, and deplored the absence of a serious market for worthy fantastic literature.[19] He also fumed in his letters about the timidity of editors, scared off by the too great horror of his tales and fearing

23

the censure of readers.[20] And yet his activities now yielded him fifteen dollars a week—a veritable fortune!

From then on he was able to travel. Secure in his permanent attachment to Providence, he returned to New York in 1928, where he met again his friends and his wife, from whom he had now obtained a divorce.[21] The following year he went to the South, and was fascinated by the civilization there. The South had a history, a homogeneous past, an identity, a *profundity*. Moreover, in Richmond there were only a few Jews, and the Negroes knew how to keep in line.[22] He was so totally enraptured by the South that he returned there in 1930, less to admire new scenery or antiquarian sites than to meet again a people who had been established there for three centuries, in an area that industrialism had by some miracle spared. The South was the last bastion of colonial America, a place where time did not exist: The people lived as they had in the beginning.[23]

His quest for origins also led him to Quebec, where for the first time he trod on British soil, in a dominion that had remained faithful to His Majesty. His joy at being able to abolish the present was complete. It was only there that he was truly happy and at ease, for he could sense under him the profundities of mythical time or, at the very least, of history. After these long journeys he returned to Providence and never left it except for brief excursions in the New England that was so dear to his heart. Always faithful to his friends—Frank Belknap Long, Clark Ashton Smith, August Derleth—he sent them interminable epistles, sprightly yet calm. Surrounded by books and cats—his continual companions, which in many places irrupt into his work[24]—he entered serenely into maturity. But Yog-Sothoth did not wish that "Theobald" attain a grandfather's age: he died at age forty-seven,[25] of duodenal cancer, and was laid to rest in his native city, into Mother Earth.

Physically Lovecraft was tall—five feet eleven inches, as Donald Wandrei tells us[26]—lean, stiff, and formal. He had an ugly hatchet face, a long and projecting chin, and a large nose. This descendant of the Teutons had black eyes and hair and fragile skin, which often gave him trouble. He complained of his appearance, which so ill accorded with his dreams and made him abnormally timid in his encounters with others. He compensated for this disagreeable physique by a great dignity in his gestures and remarks, a dignity that he would like to have thought British: ugly in spite of himself, he at least had the resourcefulness to show that he was of good birth. He suffered from various allergies; he could not tolerate the odor of tobacco and grumbled when his friends smoked. He himself never smoked except in the company of Addison, at Will's in Rupell Street at Covent Garden.[27] . . . The odor of fish made him ill, as well as anything that concerned the sea, which in his tales becomes the place of ultimate abomination. He had a well-developed olfactory sense, particularly trained to detect the stenches of the world. Lovecraft was quick to be disgusted and sickened, and his sensory repugnances, which in his work take on an oneiric fullness, are basically at the root of his aesthetic of the unclean. Very sensitive to cold, he by the same mechanism of projection turned the North and South Poles into places of terror. In "Cool Air" (1926) all the horror is concentrated in that icy room where, thanks to artificial mechanisms, a man survives who has been dead for years. Lovecraft's fantastic universe is of the same dimensions as his psyche, burdened with complexes. A psychiatrist would surely find in his letters alarming indications of neurosis, which could be analyzed, interpreted, and codified; some signs do not escape even the most naive of readers.

His precarious health—in many respects he was but an invalid—would doubtless have required a rigorous hygiene, a strict diet, and a discipline in his daily schedule. Instead, he worked at night, when the world of outer "realities" had retired into itself,[28] slept for part of the day, and fed himself on ill-prepared canned foods, ice cream, and sweets. He lived within himself, going over his dreams, outside of the world. He hated reality.[29] Human contact oppressed him, his contemporaries annoyed him, he regretted that he was not deaf.[30] Just like the character of the tale of that name, he was an "outsider." He was happy only in the dark depths of unfathomable life, where he roamed in his subterranean labyrinths with the ease of a vampire: He hated the level of clear, normal life.

Regarding women and sexuality, he was at best indifferent. What is a pretty girl? Nothing more than a mixture of carbon, hydrogen, oxygen, and nitrogen, with a little phosphorus and some other ingredients, all of which is destined promptly to disintegrate. Sex is the order of the lower instincts; it is savages and apes mating in their dark forests—no more. It is the task of man— or in any case of the "good Aryan"—to raise his eyes toward space and to define himself in terms of infinity.[31] To his friend Kleiner, who wanted to see him mix eroticism with the fantastic in his tales, he took the trouble to explain his attitude: He is hostile toward

eroticism (a) because it is an established fact that its direct manifestations are looked on with distaste by all races and all cultures;
(b) because the sexual instinct is, by all evidence, tied to base
organic phenomena; (c) because there is a patent connection between sexuality and a nation's decadence; and (d) because the
interest attached to the thing has been grossly exaggerated.[32]

Likewise, Lovecraft seriously put his young friend Belknap
Long on guard concerning the inelegance of some attitudes, and
the danger that is present, from the point of view of artistic creation, when one resorts to vulgarities; and to illustrate his thesis,
he cited Cabell's *Jurgen* and Joyce's *Ulysses*.[33] . . . This certainly
explains many things! As for him, he had from age eight pierced all
the mysteries of the human body from encyclopedias; and immediately satisfying his curiosity about the "tedious details of animal
biology,"[34] he then forever lost all interest in this question. Even
the least attentive reader will have noted that there are no women
in the Lovecraftian universe; at least, there are no women but
sorceresses, unwed mothers who give birth to monsters, or the
Asenath Waites who, under a feminine exterior, are occupied by a
redoubtable and *male* presence. . . . This also explains, perhaps,
why Lovecraft's ghouls, conforming so little to tradition, do not
suck blood—this oral aspect always having sexual implications—
but gnaw on bones or other dry matter. Doubtless there were few
who were as asexual as Lovecraft, so neutralized on the surface;
but in the depths singular monsters move.

Lovecraft's attraction for the past, which made him antedate his
letters by two centuries and, like Addison, write with the long *s*,
had unexpected consequences in his political views. England remained for him his true country; he severely condemned what he
called the "Yankee sedition," or, again, the "treason of 1775–
83."[35] He always considered Providence a "Royal Plantation" and
New England "His Majesty's Province." His wife tells us that all
his life he considered himself a "displaced Englishman."[36]

Up to this, nothing was wrong. But to be of "undiluted
Englishry"[37] meant that he in a way had to adopt the theories of the
far right. The war revealed him as a militarist in the extreme. Unable
to fight, his health rendering him unsuitable for service, he vituper-
ated the apathy and cowardice of his contemporaries, and wished
that they would assert a little more of their "ancient Teutonic
brutality."[38] From 1915 on, he edited and published an amateur
journal, *The Conservative*, in which he violently took the pacifists to

task and spiritedly preached "Pan-Saxonism," that is, "the domination by the English and kindred races over the lesser divisions of mankind."[39] The Irish question inspired bitter remarks from him about the Sinn Fein.[40] The Ku Klux Klan, on the other hand, was for him a "noble . . . band of Southerners who saved half of the country from destruction at the close of the Civil War."[41] The October Revolution confirmed his violent aversion for the "Socialist lie" and "the dictatorship of the proletariat."[42]

The advent of fascism in Europe found him warmly sympathetic: He had been discussing it with Galpin since 1923, and had told James F. Morton of the contempt in which he held the mob. Democracy is a sure sign of the decadence and regression of nations. We must, he said, quickly reject all liberalism, vigorously denounce the illusion of progress, and impose a strict social and political order. The ideal would be the unification of the English and the "true" Americans to form a new empire and to impose their domination on the world.[43] His wife tells us that he heartily admired Hitler and read *Mein Kampf* in one gulp upon its appearance in an English translation.[44] To this influence she attributed Lovecraft's hatred for Jews and the ethnic minorities of the country. In fact, there was in this invalid the worship of the Viking, in this spineless man the veneration of the blond-haired, blue-eyed warrior, and a real or simulated taste for brutality and violence: "The one sound power in the world," he wrote, "is the power of a hairy muscular right arm."[45] To be English is to belong to a "superior race"; it is to be neither Negro nor Jew nor Latin.

But Lovecraft was a racist well before he read *Mein Kampf.* In an unpublished poem which dates from 1905,[46] the adolescent is already denouncing the blind zeal of the North, which waged an impious war on the South, the sole pretext being the servitude of colored people. But happily man's madness has its limits and nature its laws: by the thousands, the "savage black, the aperesembling beast," ought surely to be exterminated. We may excuse this remark by the extreme youth of the author; but seven years later, at age twenty-two, he gave evidence of the same violence in another short poem, where he explained how God had created the Negro halfway, on the scale of beings, between man and beast.[47]

He was entirely in favor of the most rigorous forms of segregation, at least in public transport and on the beaches. Why cannot it be applied in New York as it was in the South? Imagine, he wrote

in 1925 to Mrs. Gamwell when she was visiting Florida, the re-
action of a sensitive person who bathes in the company of "greasy
chimpanzees"! The only thing that makes life endurable in those
areas where there are many Negroes is the principle of Jim Crow.
Let's keep them from our sight, or massacre them all, so that a
white man can walk the streets without being nauseated.[48] What
bitter disappointment was his when, while on a trip to Pelham Bay
Park, he found himself amid a dense crowd, nine-tenths of which
was composed of Negroes! These flabby, smelling, grimacing "entities" so stirred his heart that he literally called for help.[49]

If he was not kindly disposed toward Negroes, he was hardly
more indulgent toward Italians, Poles, Orientals, and the represen-
tatives of other "inferior races" whom he passed daily on the
streets of New York and even (supreme horror!) in the streets of
Providence. The menace of the Orientals that hung over the world
was faraway, so that it worried him only indifferently. Doubtless it
would one day be necessary to exterminate Japan and take arms
against China, but it would be a day in which he would have no
part.[50] Still, their presence was, in some quarters, traumatic.
"Chinatown," which he visited in 1922 with Kleiner, upset him
greatly:

> My gawd—what a filthy dump! I thought Providence had slums,
> and antique Bostonium as well; but damn me if I ever saw anything
> like the sprawling sty-atmosphere of N.Y.'s lower East Side. We
> walked—at my suggestion—in the middle of the street, for contact
> with the heterogeneous sidewalk denizens, spilled out of their bulg-
> ing brick kennels as if by a spawning beyond the capability of the
> places, was not to be sought. At times, though, we struck peculiarly
> deserted areas—these swine have instinctive swarming movements,
> no doubt, which no ordinary biologist can fathom. Gawd knows
> what they are— . . . —a bastard mess of stewing mongrel flesh
> without intellect, repellent to eye, nose, and imagination—would to
> heaven a kindly gust of cyanogen could asphyxiate the whole gigan-
> tic abortion, end the misery, and clean out the place.[51]

He was so shocked by this visit that two years later he told the
same tale to Frank Belknap Long, in terms at least as virulent:

> The organic things—Italo-Semitico-Mongoloid—inhabiting that
> awful cesspool could not by any stretch of the imagination be call'd
> human. They were monstrous and nebulous adumbrations of the

pithecanthropoid and amoebal; vaguely moulded from some stink-
ing viscous slime of earth's corruption, and slithering and oozing in
and on the filthy streets or in and out of windows and doorways in a
fashion suggestive of nothing but infesting worms or deep-sea un-
namabilities. They—or the degenerate gelatinous fermentation of
which they were composed—seem'd to ooze, seep and trickle thro'
the gaping cracks in the horrible houses . . . and I thought of some
avenue of Cyclopean and unwholesome vats, crammed to the
vomiting point with gangrenous vileness, and about to burst and
inundate the world in one leprous cataclysm of semi-fluid rotten-
ness. From that nightmare of perverse infection I could not carry
away the memory of any living face. The individually grotesque was
lost in the collectively devastating; which left on the eye only the
broad, phantasmal lineaments of the morbid soul of disintegration
and decay . . . a yellow leering mask with sour, sticky, acid ichors
oozing at eyes, ears, nose, and mouth, and abnormally bubbling
from monstrous and unbelievable sores at every point. . . .[52]

These brief extracts are not in any sense exceptional; we could
cite many others, all as revealing. They suffice, however, in showing how Lovecraft *dreamed his repugnances* and with what verbal
richness he ranted from purely sensory data. In him, art was nourished by neurosis—it furnished him with his materials; but that art
allowed him to sublimate the horror, to extract from it its quintessence, and through it, perhaps, to cure his neurosis. We thus touch
already upon the heart of the problem in Lovecraft's fantastic creation, where the hideous monsters are in large part merely the
projection, in the "dark chamber" of a sick mind, of obsessive
images that his political and racial vision of the American world
had given him.

About Jews he was more tolerant, because he recognized in
them a possibility of integration that he refused to other ethnic
groups. Still, he declared that this assimilation must take place
according to certain modes and in proper—that is, infinitesimal—
proportions. He refused to admit that the Hebraic culture, essentially exotic and oriental, would one day force itself to be recognized and to claim a place in the Western world. For indeed, the
ignominious history of the Jews during the past two thousand
years, when they were placed prostrate and made to lick the boots
of their oppressors, did not encourage indulgence. Were they not,
moreover, responsible for the spiritual corruption of the country,
they who had given the world this crucified madman before whom

the crowd knelt? Whereas it would be much better to yell and laugh to Thor or Odin, Lovecraft, the "blond Teuton soul," was sickened to death by this. Of course, to be assimilated without danger into Aryan society, the Jew must consent to divest himself of his heavy cultural and religious heritage to assume his new character.[53] The "good Jews" whom he knew and honored with his friendship, such as Samuel Loveman, were all molded from the Hellenic culture and thus constituted the proof of this possible conversion.

He did not hold it as less true that the Teutonic race, the *Aryan* race, was the "cream of humanity,"[54] and that he himself had the rare privilege of belonging to it. He declared himself essentially a "Teuton and a barbarian," a Nordic son of Odin, brother of Hengist and Horsa, ready to drink the hot blood of his enemies in the freshly hollowed-out skull of a Celt.[55] If we are to believe this, we may have to forget the New York episode of his life when he threw away the mousetraps after each use to avoid touching the *corpus dilecti!*[56]

Which of these categorical opinions were a pose and which a result of deep conviction? It is hard to say. But whatever answer we give to this difficult question, it is not without interest, for the sake of the rest of this study, to show even now that Lovecraft *dreamed himself* a blond giant with blue eyes and willed himself politically a "Tory, Czarist, Junker, patrician, Fascist, oligarchist, nationalist, [and] militarist."[57]

He is more to be pitied than blamed. His racism, like his political extremism, was a direct consequence of his philosophical views, which were totally nihilistic. We are astonished that he even took the time and trouble to express his distaste so vigorously, for he felt that nothing ultimately is of any great importance.[58] Life is hollow and futile, and we are going adrift on a sea that no one has ever charted. Bred totally on Democritus and Lucretius, on Leucippus and Epicurus, on Schopenhauer and Nietzsche, on Darwin and Huxley, he produced, for himself and for his correspondents, a bizarre synthesis of ancient mechanistic philosophy, German pessimism, and the most rigorous positivist materialism.

Born in a Puritan milieu, he began by ridding himself of God. He tells us in a letter to Moe[59] how, when very young, he was exasperated by Puritan doctrine and how rapidly he persuaded himself not to have any religious fiber. Too many questions pressed on his young, critical mind; and the theologians—those men who reason by question-begging and who invent what they do not know—had too many ready-made answers and were too ready to condemn.[60]

In effect, the Judeo-Christian mythology *has absolutely no truth,*[61] and if the precepts of Christ were ever applied to the letter, they would lead only to anarchy and the collapse of all cultural values:[62] they are in themselves nefarious and pernicious. Everything in the Scriptures is myth and fable, and can be explained rationally if one considers the agonies and aspirations of primitive man, quick to invest his "dream self"—the part of himself that in his dreams escapes him—with transcendency and immortality. This belief is perpetuated from age to age for various reasons, all of them human, of which the principal ones are the desire for conformity and a blind respect for tradition.[63] It is, however, good that it be thus: Religious principles constitute an indispensable yoke for the herd and impose on them a salutary moral order. But no one who has read Frazer can possibly have the least faith in these things, which are mere legends. . . .

Having discarded the obstacle of God, Lovecraft could now logically establish his absolute nihilism. For him, humanity has evolved aimlessly and absurdly; it is no more than a minute point in the unsoundable abysms of time and space. The appearance of the human race constitutes only a negligible incident in the endless history of the Cosmos.[64] Man is but an infinitesimal fragment of that cosmic mass of matter on which fickle and capricious forces act.[65] The Cosmos itself exists only by the incessant redistribution of the electrons composing it. All things are the accidental results of inessential causes. Nothing indicates that somewhere there is an aim, an end, a *center.*[66] Lovecraft had vainly probed space and, like the good "agnostic monist" that he was, found at the end of his quest nothing but a ceaseless disintegration and reconstruction of atoms and molecules, an absurd game of forces each mutually dependent on the other, a game that has always existed and will always exist.[67]

Lovecraft wrote, in a collective letter to his friends Kleiner, Cole, and Moe, that he could not see how a thoughtful man could ever be happy.[68] Indeed, he could hardly have been happy himself, and this explains a good many of his disagreeable remarks. Without doubt he was—all his life, in the most total and dramatic sense of the term—a *man without hope.* From this one can understand his apathy, his skepticism concerning the laughable initiatives that this so-called game of cosmic forces leaves up to the individual. Because "crystals, colloids, metals, protozoa, men, molecules, etherwaves, [and] baboons"[69] are the same from the point of view of their relations with the infinities of space and time, what good is it to try to do anything? We understand also that he had seriously and frequently considered putting himself to death; suicide, outside the Judeo-Christian tradition, is a common gesture sometimes useful to accomplish. When we read Lovecraft's fantastic tales it is important to remember this conception of the world: to what extent is fiction an ironic and oblique commentary on the profound reality of things? Are not these characters, these playthings of forces—the cruel and absurd Gods—which infinitely overshadow them simply Lovecraft himself, trapped as he was by his readings and his total despair? The fantastic, after all, is perhaps nothing more than a heartrending revelation of the absurd, seeking to dislodge the reader from his normal states of mind and his familiar certitudes. . . .

If Lovecraft never actually killed himself, we may believe that it was because of his dreams, which transported him to another world where horror was indeed present but was to an extent controllable. The dreams that he drew upon came at first from books. However original was, in many respects, the fantastic creation of "Pappos Nekrophilos," as he liked to call himself,[70] it is nonetheless vital not to neglect the many purely literary influences that acted on him.

In the first rank we must cite Poe, the model, the idol, the archetype,[71] whom he unhesitatingly placed at the summit of all fantastic literature.[72] His shade hovered forever and ever over the streets, roofs, and cemeteries of Providence. Always did Lovecraft try, in his personal comportment as well as in his tales, to identify himself with the man who had written what he held to be an absolute masterpiece, "The Fall of the House of Usher." He carried this veneration so far as sometimes to sign his letters "H: Poe Lovecraft."[73]

After Poe, whom he had read since the age of seven, came Lord Dunsany, whom he always considered the greatest master of dreams, and whom he discovered somewhat tardily, in 1919. But what was his joy at entering this subtly decadent universe, where life and the world were presented to the reader as being merely the fragile dreams of archaic Gods! That unreal atmosphere, that sublimation of the emotions, that antiquated aestheticism that characterizes *The Book of Wonder, The Gods of Pegāna*, or *The Sword of Welleran* flattered his taste for poetic reverie, and at the same time the astonishingly precise and fantastically beautiful drawings of S. H. Sime stimulated his imagination. "Dunsany," he wrote in 1923, "has influenced me more than anyone else except Poe—his rich language, his cosmic point of view, his remote dream-world, & his exquisite sense of the fantastic all appeal to me more than anything else in modern literature. My first encounter with him—in the autumn of 1919—gave an immense impetus to my writing; perhaps the greatest it has ever had."[74]

Next came Machen, the "Titan," perhaps the greatest living *fantaisiste* according to Lovecraft. What somber grandeur is in his stories of other times, in his tales that plunge their roots into the most archaic layers of Celtic history! Tales full of horror, too, which surges brusquely from the depths, founded on the superstitious beliefs of a people who through the centuries have preserved their sense of mystery and the numinous. And is *The Hill of Dreams* not a little like Lovecraft's hill, the inspired mount from which he dominated the roofs of Providence and the world? Lovecraft entered into immediate sympathy with a spirit profoundly enrooted in a secular tradition and culture, in the folklore of a great people.

He also knew well the other masters of fantastic literature. He even wrote an important study of the subject,[75] where he spoke of the English Gothic novelists, of Hoffmann, Bierce, Marion Crawford, John Buchan, M. R. James, and others, in terms that allow us to suppose he had read them seriously and voluminously. Lovecraft was not a pure dreamer, a naive *fantaisiste:* he had carefully studied the genre before renewing it. But no writers enticed or influenced him as much as Poe, Machen, and Dunsany: these three had, as he confided to one of his correspondents,[76] already said all that he had to say; and he added sadly, "There are my 'Poe' pieces & my 'Dunsany' pieces—but alas—where are any *Lovecraft* pieces?"[77] Such modesty and sadness—possibly feigned—are, we think, not proper. Lovecraft in his own right had clear, personal, and original notions despite what he would say. And his work, for all its flagrant defects, is different from all others.

His remarks on the technique of writing have the utmost bearing on the profound significance of his work. He frequently insisted on the importance of *images*, confirming by this the role that, in fantastic creation, is played by the sensory element. He tells us that he wrote to fix and preserve some fleeting images that suddenly haunted him and fell immediately away into the night. Perhaps it was also to exorcise them. . . . But let us not anticipate. These images of dream must be captured in such a way as to be understandable to all. These images, these carriers of anguish, should communicate fear, and should certainly suggest what in the eyes of the author was the essence of the fantastic—the obsessive presence of the Unknown, which can at any instant surge from the gulfs, from beyond the "Edge of the World." . . . The absolute criterion for the weird is this subtle and progressive intrusion of the Invisible, of the Inconceivable, into our familiar world, an intrusion that should be more suggested than described, by a fine, transparent system of adequate signs and clues. It is entirely a question of atmosphere; horror thrives on the undefined.

But the fantastic is not only a technique; in Lovecraft it responded to a need for mystery and horror. It partly filled the void that his agnosticism and despair had carved in him. "Somehow," he wrote,

> I cannot become truly interested in anything which does not suggest incredible marvels just around the corner—glorious and ethereal cities of golden roofs and marble terraces beyond the sunset, or vague, dim cosmic presences clawing ominously at the thin rim where the known universe meets the outer and fathomless abyss. The world and all its inhabitants impress me as immeasurably insignificant, so that I always crave intimations of larger and subtler symmetries than those which concern mankind.[78]

The fantastic "just around the corner," the marvels available in the very heart of our environment, correspond in Lovecraft to an attempt at sublimating the world, the only thing capable of giving him an ephemeral serenity. Here the techniques of the writer and the methods of the dreamer join, in a quest for that "absolute reality" hidden behind the illusory data of the senses.[79] It is this mysterious, ever inaccessible presence that Lovecraft with a pathetic stubbornness pursued in his diurnal and nocturnal dreams. It is from this that he drew the strength to survive; it is this that he tried to fix by a series of approximate images. It is because of this that he was, in the eyes of men and in his own eyes, an "outsider."

2

DWELLINGS AND LANDSCAPES

I am above all *scenic and architectural* in my tastes.

—Lovecraft[1]

With few exceptions, the Lovecraftian universe is circumscribed in a well-determined region of the United States. It is a closed space, cut off from the rest of the country and the world, a different place, another province, a privileged corner of the cosmos where the outer forces and the powers from beyond the world can, by some mysterious favor, freely manifest themselves.

This choice world is New England, the land of origins, of the first beginnings, the Promised Land of mythical times, where the American nation was born and from which it thrust out its fleshly roots. No other place in the United States could better lend itself to the irruption of the bizarre. By its very nature the fantastic is manifested most efficaciously where a historic profundity is embedded under the surface of everyday life.

New England was also Lovecraft's native soil, the only point on earth with which he could totally identify. This obscure emotion of belonging, of rootedness, was for him the primordial condition of all plenitude. He tells us that his vital force, like that of Antaeus, depends strictly on contact with the Mother Earth who bore him.[2] Everyone knows that we dream well only when living in that absolutely intimate region of our childhood: Only the "natal home" can be changed into a dream-dwelling.

New England is the province of marvelous cities that Lovecraft so often visited and so dearly loved: Providence, Boston, Marblehead, Salem, Newport. In those cities the past surfaces and affirms itself at each street corner, and all the homes have a single history; it is a place of *profound towns*, rooted in the homogeneous tradition of Puritanism and the culture of a single race. What a difference from New York, where the verticality of the skyscraper is only an exterior dimension! Instead of being rooted in the earth, these dwellings spurt out vertiginously toward the sky. This is a place devoid of a center or an identity or ties with the past,[3] a city to which none of the many ethnic groups composing it really belong. Then again, New England has its own folklore, its own legends, which belong to racial memory: the tales of sorcery, impious cults, and diabolical rites that are as a faraway family heritage, the legacy of the Old Ones.

These cities through which Lovecraft loved to stroll are also ports, oriented toward the old continent, toward the past. These ports give on to the great open sea, on unknown immensity, whence *anything could come:* the blue line on the horizon that represents the famous "Edge of the World" so dear to Dunsany, beyond which the unsoundable and terrifying abysms of dream might lurk.

New England, with its deep forests, its marvelous landscapes, its wild mountains, its rugged coast gouged with gulfs, is certainly a place with a potential for adventure and mystery. To walk there, says Lovecraft, is to cross time and space as if penetrating a picture hung on a wall, to settle into the inadmissible; nowhere else is it possible so strongly to sense the presence of the bizarre, the sinister, the unholy, the macabre.[4] In this predestined framework, in this elect land, where the equivocal and the aleatory preside over man's rapports with nature, almost all Lovecraft's tales unfold.

It is a world whose *reality*—physical, topographical, historical—should be emphasized. It is well known that the truly fantastic exists only where the impossible can make an irruption, through time and space, into an objectively familiar locale.

And yet, there is a city very dear to the author's heart for which we vainly search on a map—antique Arkham, haunted by the evil spells of the past, with its roofs bent by the weight of centuries, its gables and its balustrades of another age, its narrow and tortuous streets. There is a port where no vessel of any known nationality has ever touched—Innsmouth. And there is a hamlet lost in western Massachusetts, which no traveler today can ever reach—Dunwich. These imaginary places form, in the real topography of New England, a zone of shadow, a zone of mystery, a *dream-zone*, which spreads little by little to the rest of the countryside, contaminating the diurnal space of the maps and charts and giving it a suddenly different aspect. The familiarity of places is blurred, leaving the weird to take its place. Arkham is at once Boston and Newport, Providence and Salem, Portsmouth and Marblehead—a point in mythical space toward which dreams converge and where all the accumulated images gathered in the course of Lovecraft's interminable walks are superimposed. Arkham is, in the most precise sense of the term, a structure condensed from dreams, around which is built and organized an entire universe of inexpressible wonders and blasphemous horrors. Arkham and its vicinity are, in the Lovecraftian topography, the fault through which the bizarre, the horrific, the disquieting, the morbid, and the unclean spread. In the heart of the American world, at a laughably short distance from the great industrial centers, from the most respected universities, from the tourist sites—amid smiling civilization—Lovecraft sets up an abominable region where unbelievable evils are practiced.

In this region, the picturesque landscapes of New England are degraded, corrupted from the effects of mysterious forces from beyond. After the fall of a strange meteorite, in "The Colour out of Space," no trace of vegetation remains on the fields; the effect of the bizarre is manifested by a profound withering. In the circumference of this zone, the scrawny trees, as if struck by lightning, waste away, the grass becomes gray, the rocks crumble. Elsewhere, as if nature were unhinged, forests suddenly become denser, darker. Perspective itself is distorted—it is as if we have found ourselves in a landscape from the canvas of that master of the picturesque, Salvator Rosa.[5]

In "The Lurking Fear," the soil is covered by a fetid and corrupt vegetation, a poisonous mold representing a type of horrible suppuration of the earth; the trees, infested by an unspeakable essence they draw from this decay, take on grotesque and demented forms. Decrepitude, corruption settle wherever the supernatural has intruded. The Lovecraftian fantastic is manifestly *decadent:* The bizarre does not fall from space to terrify or confound, but to corrupt. It is a type of gangrene that gnaws, wears away, and finally rots the familiar world through and through.

The strain obviously spreads to architecture, a choice constituent of these degraded landscapes. The old colonial homes dear to Lovecraft's heart, with their irregular gables, their bizarre framework, their transomed windows—all the residences of another age that incite meditation and dream—become through dream sinister places where nameless abominations rule. Innumerable are the dwellings that, baleful and menacing, loom on the horizon in Lovecraft's tales; sometimes they are rooted in the earth by an inextricable network of subterranean tunnels or peopled with swarming horrors;[6] sometimes they are perched, conversely, on a remote cliff in the mist thousands of feet above the waves, with a door opening on to the void as the only possible entrance.[7] Sometimes cracked and unwholesome like Poe's, sometimes unreal and faraway like Dunsany's, they are the setting of foul practices, of barbarous banquets at which human flesh may well be featured on the menu; they are evil places haunted by phosphorescent, gelatinous, and vampiric entities who have malevolently assimilated the flesh and souls of their unfortunate tenants.

The dwelling is a fantastic place par excellence, insofar as it demarcates and isolates the malefic region in a particularly adequate way. It materializes the mythical threshold that makes possible the necessary transgressions and justifies the inevitable retribution: The horror it inspires is primordial and brings up in each individual the most archaic layers of racial memory. The same irrepressible anguish seizes all the characters the moment they cross the forbidden portico, knowing confusedly that they are performing the irremediable and are binding themselves irreversibly. Being the meeting place of the here and the beyond, all the houses are in a way fateful. Lovecraft cannot bring the abnormal to his hero except within the interior of these tragic walls, which enclose, contain, and up to a point dam up the irrational. To enter one of these old edifices of New England is to accept the discovery there of unheard-of forms of life, of beings that attain their monstrous fullness only insofar as their confinement preserves and maintains their essential difference. Vampires, shoggoths, and mutants, incubi, lemurs, and Aegypans are their true selves only in their original settings. All thresholds are, in essence, forbidden. To cross them is at the same time to expose the unholy, for the incomprehensible, in an advanced society that has definitively broken off with the mystical, is necessarily a form of Evil. How many sabbaths, how many Walpurgis-nights, how many blasphemous rites have for their settings these picturesque and many-gabled homes! Erected on the native soil, contemporaneous with the earliest days of the nation, they are for Lovecraft structures of oneiric exploration, guiding dream along the vertical axis that they delineate, down to the vertiginous abysms of space and time. The inquiry conducted by the narrator of "The Shunned House" makes him descend, generation by generation, into the hidden depths of American history where horror is encountered. Gilman, in "The Dreams in the Witch House," is compelled to dream by the architecture of the room he inhabits, and is driven to explore an immaterial cosmos of strange and alarming marvels.

Lovecraft's homes are the vehicles of dream, the irreplaceable auxiliaries of the imaginary, which permit the author to root his work in a geographically individualized secular tradition. Descending to the cellar, the hero is driven into a national past and finds, at the foot of the spiral staircase that vertically structures the whole edifice, the folklore of the Beginning. Infallibly, the ever descending steps lead the dreamer to myth.

The man who dated his letters as from the "Usual Sepulchre"[8] enjoyed, like Poe, haunting old cemeteries.[9] His nostalgia, his taste for the mossy vestiges of other times, and, we must say, the morbid vein of his temperament, drove him often to sit and dream on a tomb with time-effaced inscriptions. Cemeteries belong entirely to bygone times; to visit them is to leave intolerable reality and flee toward immaterial horizons where life is more real, more full, because all there is already done. In a word, it is to feign death.

In many of his tales we find the old cemeteries of Providence, Boston, and Marblehead, but they do not have the diurnal aspect Lovecraft gives them in his letters. Metamorphosed by oneiric composition, they suddenly become places where the latent horror that they inspire is *reactivated*. By day, on the level of clear life, a tomb is only a raised sign on the smooth surface of the present. In the night of dream, the sign is inversed and the tumulus becomes a hole, a pit, a receptacle where unclean osmoses and repugnant transformations take place. From the melancholy vestige that it was, the tomb becomes a *functional place*. The crypts are then hollowed out alarmingly, reaching incredible depths and stretching toward the bottom by way of subterranean tunnels, which push simultaneously into the earth and into the past. Then, by these imaginary conduits, from the most archaic layers of subsoil and time, the Abominable, the Unnameable can resurface. Cemeteries are, in Lovecraft's works, privileged places where terror surfaces; the sepulchers are so many gaping orifices to the *underneath*, which is a type of *beyond*. After having read "The Statement of Randolph Carter," we can never again forget the story of that insane expedition organized by Warren in the depths of a peculiarly redoubtable crypt: Descending to the bottom of the gulf, he stayed in telephone contact with the surface up to the moment the voice which Carter heard in the receiver . . . was no longer that of his friend.

Scientists also lurk in cemeteries, though in a more conventional way: These are special searchers who need special materials for their experiments. Such is Joseph Curwen, who, from the "essential Saltes" of which cadavers are composed, makes the spirits of the dead appear.[10] Such is Herbert West, who fragmentarily reanimates the still "worthwhile" parts of human remnants so as to make new and monstrous beings from them.[11] Or again, there are the young esthetes of horror, the "neurotic virtuosi"[12] who freely profane sepulchers to extract unclean trophies. Then comes the night when, forcing a tomb inhabited by a particularly redoubtable presence, they pay for their mad audacity. In Lovecraft, cemeteries always become what they by no means ought to be: *animated* places where disquieting exchanges between the world of the surface and the gulf take place.

The final element in the Lovecraftian landscape is the sea. Although the tourist may like to dream next to it in the charming ports of New England, it is never a friendly, familiar element for our writer. It also has its depths, more unsoundable, more primordial than even those of the earth, concealing nauseous horrors. It is inhabited by monsters who menace the peace of mankind and pull men in after them into their original element. Nothing is more abominable than a Deep One—unless it be, perhaps, the deity they adore, Dagon, that gigantic, scaly, and viscous entity, the mere sight of which makes lost navigators lose their reason.[13] It does not do to explore the bottom of these liquid abysms. Strange temples are raised there where barbarous rites are performed,[14] and incredibly ancient cities are there, engulfed for millennia but always, it seems, inhabited, where singular sacrifices are made. Carter, leaning over the rails of the sailboat conveying him to Oriab, perceives at the bottom of the transparent waters the body of a sailor bound upside down to a monolith—a sailor who no longer has eyes.[15]

Sometimes, in the course of some geologic upheaval, there emerges from the depths one or the other of the underwater cities. But when it happens to be the dead city of R'lyeh, built millions of years before the beginning of history, then madness must await the human race. For R'lyeh is the city where, in an edifice whose architectural norms defy the human mind, Cthulhu himself rests. As long as one sees the Great Old One, this deity who came from the stars in immemorial times, only in the approximate reproductions carved in rock by his primitive admirers, one still has a chance to survive. But when the god himself—this veritable moving mountain, this hideous contradiction of all the laws of nature, this indescribable "cosmic entity" emerging from the waves— draws up, then . . . death is the supreme—nay, only—refuge. "When I think of the *extent* of all that may be brooding down there," says the narrator of "The Call of Cthulhu," "I almost wish to kill myself forthwith."[16]

Such, then, is the setting where, for a paltry instant, the imperceptible silhouettes of Lovecraft's characters move. It is a setting strangely familiar and fabulously faraway, where a dream-topography is superimposed on the real topography. Geographic space is substituted by a malefic space. The landscape, the cities, the dwellings of New England lose their pleasant, picturesque, diurnal aspect, to become lunatic sites, nocturnal images, degraded images of a demented dream.

About the characters themselves we must say a word. They are for the most part eminently respectable individuals, descended from the oldest families in New England: university professors—of that celebrated Miskatonic University, which, in the author's dream, represents Brown University—reputed doctors, worthies surrounded by general consideration. All lead active, peaceful, useful lives in the heart of their community, until the day when, in their sheltered existence, the bizarre monstrously surges. By the place they occupy in society, however, they represent an elite. Holders of culture, they profess the absolute skepticism that is the attribute of their class: about the supernatural, they all have the same attitude of perfect incredulity as Lovecraft. Although the lessers around whom they lead their inquiries—the degenerate peasants of the Catskills or the decadent populace of the cities— are open to all superstitions and to the most bizarre ideas, they preserve, or try to preserve, their lucidity and their cold reason to the end. In Lovecraft's tales they embody what it would be tempting to call the "function of rationality"—an essential, irreplaceable element in all fantastic creation, because it gives the scale of the real, the measure of the waking world. They are in their way an integral part of the landscape, representing waking characters who move in a dream-setting. It is because they are all reasonable men in a demented world that the Lovecraftian fantastic is totally efficacious. These savants, these doctors, these professors, being close to the reader, are the guarantee of the impossible.

Finally, it is manifest that many of them are projections of the author himself, who through the illusion of literature thus enters his own imaginary world. The phenomenon has, as we will see, its importance. Like Lovecraft, Charles Dexter Ward was born in Providence, where he passed a studious adolescence in the shadow of the John Hay Library. Like him, he had an exclusive passion for his native town, with its steeples, its sunlit roofs, and its tortuous streets. Like him particularly, he liked to wander into the old parts of town, admire the old colonial houses, and dream of the past, for it is to Charles Dexter Ward that "something will happen." . . . Analogously, the narrator of "He" begins his story with the words: "My coming to New York was a mistake . . . ,"[17] and the reader is soon made to understand, by the way he speaks of that dead city where soulless and repulsive automata move about, that the narrator is no other than the author himself. And it is he who, just around the corner, will encounter adventure. We also recognize Lovecraft in the traits of Edward Derby, in "The Thing on the Doorstep," in that he is an only child, with fragile health and morbid temperament, and so sheltered by his parents that he cannot make any decisions by himself. Through weakness he will also marry a woman with whom he is ill-matched. Therefore, it is on him, and no other, that horror will pounce. . . .

We are then justified, it seems, in wondering whether these characters do not, regarding the author, play a vicarious role:

Through them Lovecraft gives the bizarre to himself, by a series of ordeals that strangely recall the initiation stages of yore. The sites, the landscapes, the dwellings that we have noted become then the privileged terrain of a mythical quest, the nocturnal place where, gropingly and amid unspeakable horrors, this devotee of genealogy searches for his own identity.

3

THE METAMORPHOSES OF SPACE

They told him that every figure of space is but the result of the intersection by a plane of some corresponding figure of one more dimension—as a square is cut from a cube or a circle from a sphere. The cube and sphere, of three dimensions, are thus cut from corresponding forms of four dimensions that men know only through guesses and dreams; and these in turn are cut from forms of five dimensions, and so on up to the dizzy and reachless heights of archetypal infinity.

—"Through the Gates of the Silver Key"[1]

It is a well-known fact that disorder is at the very source of the fantastic. This suspension of natural laws can be manifested, as far as space is concerned, only by an alteration of perspective and proportion. What in particular gives the etchings of Piranesi their disquieting beauty is the disproportion between those gigantic pillars, those measureless vaults, those endless stairways, and the insignificant silhouettes that here and there show a dwarfed humanity.

In Lovecraft, space is most profoundly altered by his oneiric vision of the world. The disordering of perspective is a phenomenon that affects the *surface,* an anomaly which above all concerns the art of the etcher or painter. When the space of the dreamer breaks down, it becomes far more alarming; its very substance is broken, its profound reality is affected.

The city, insofar as it is one of the places where space is most strongly condensed and structured, is in this regard the fantastic site par excellence. The more space is organized, the more it incites dream and calls for the compensations of the irrational. If there is a favorite motif in fantasy, it is that of the *ville double:* the real city, the diurnal city, with its streets, its bridges, its churches—the city of the maps and charts—which suddenly blurs, dissolves in an opaque mist. On its site is left a dream city—certainly as real, but black, malefic. It is a theme used by many writers—by Jean Ray in "La Ruelle tenebreuse"—but which Lovecraft treated in his own incomparable manner.

The narrator of "He" tells us how, after having been thrilled by the vision he had had of New York by twilight, he became horribly disillusioned when he explored the city by the cruel light of day. He then saw only the dirty streets infested with dark-skinned strangers, the evil and gigantic dwellings stricken with elephantiasis. Close to nausea, he chose to go out only by night, at an hour when the darkness permitted him to invent the setting of his walks.[2] In other words, he rejected—because, we note in passing, of the repugnance inspired in him by beings who were not of his race—the New York of day, monstrously rational, the horrible New York of daily promiscuity, to place himself, in the course of his long nocturnal strolls, deliberately *in a dream-situation.*

From that time on, anything became possible. He walked in the footsteps of his strange guide, slid by narrow gaps between the brick walls, threaded corridors, took a narrow vaulted passage he sometimes had to follow by crawling along sinuous bends.[3] Inevitably the labyrinthine dream came to represent an escape from the familiar world. One can arrive at "the other world" only at the end of a long, twisted path and only after having effected some oneiric circumvolutions. One ought first to lose oneself, to attain and go beyond a point of no return, to achieve the outer reaches of dream.

The entry of the principal character of "The Festival" into immaterial Kingsport, which parallels the real city, is still slower, still more progressive. To be exact, the narrator is at the start already *in* the dream city, but the reader takes note of the fact only gradually, as the narrator advances along the "endless labyrinths of steep, narrow, crooked streets"[4] that are to lead him to the home for which he searches. He had consulted a map, he says, before his trip, and knew his way. He is struck, however, by the deserted aspect of the place. There is not the least trace of footsteps in the snow, not the least cry of a child or the sound of a bell on this Christmas day. He plunges with muffled steps into a spongy world where only hazy forms and unclear silhouettes subsist, enveloped in a great silence that reigns over the inner spaces.

We find in "The Music of Erich Zann" the same parallel world that doubles common space and time. The city now in question is French. Is it perhaps Paris, which Lovecraft visited "in a dream, with Poe"?[5] The tale begins, significantly, with this sentence: "I have examined maps of the city with the greatest care, yet have never found the Rue d'Auseil." Evidently it is a dream street, which juts over a bridge of *black* rock on a *dark* river. "It was always shadowy," the author adds, "along that river, as if the smoke of neighboring factories shut out the sun perpetually."[6]

In this almost material penumbra, which constitutes a natural element of dream, the author has erected an appropriate decor for his tale: The Rue d'Auseil is steeply sloping, inaccessible to all vehicles, and broken off here and there by stairways. It is a *road without an exit*, which leads to a *blind wall*. The houses that border on it are tall, strange, irregular, worthy of the pen of a Gustave Doré. The few people who haunt it are abnormally silent and incredibly aged. In this nameless city, as in Kingsport or New York, the characters belong to a bygone, prodigiously faraway age. They also move in an unreal atmosphere, outside the sphere of real time.

In these three tales, as in several others, the real city has no other function than to lead to the dream city, much more rich, more picturesque, more frightening than the anonymous and neutral setting of our daily actions. Dream restores meaning to the houses and streets, reactivates the primordial anguish that in Lovecraft is always tied to the exploration of the past; in the land of sorcerers, horror is never far away. The act of fantasy consists precisely in lightly erasing the present. Then, behind the common, uniform, and reassuring decor of the city of today, tottering houses are built, narrow streets are laid, strange landscapes are transparently drawn, outlining another space, a fabulous "outside" on which weigh the curses of yesteryear. Myth reanimates the dead and cold cities of the contemporary world and repeoples the metropolises of the twentieth century with redoubtable entities. At the very heart of the geometrical and rational space of modern times Lovecraft installs a magical space, a forbidden realm, which restores meaning and content to the idea of *transgression,* long out of date. No; New England's past is not dead, the evil things of elder times are not entirely gone. The unholy actions, the sabbaths of yore, are perpetuated, but in a parallel space, both prodigiously faraway and dangerously close. A trifle can make us tip over; chance alone, or some perverse force, can place us in such a propitious place that suddenly we fall into the pit.

Ever is the transfer placed under the sign of black magic. This beyond-the-"edge-of-the-world" we daily skirt is a corrupted space where sacrilegious cults prevail, chanting blasphemies. Revolting sacrifices occur there. One risks the loss of one's reason, life, salvation. In the sinister and immaterial dwellings raised there, it is as if time is suspended. Sometimes their windows give out on to a colonial New York, idyllic and charming, sometimes on to a New York millennia to come, in a chaos of demented architecture where blasphemous, yellow-headed beings move furiously. Evil is embodied only by colored people. Or again, there shines, on the other side of the window, not the friendly light of any city, but there gapes the utter and opaque void of infinite space, vibrating in unison with the viol of Erich Zann—of that lifeless body whose jerking cadences, while the bow tears out chords of unholy dissonances, assume a diabolic significance, evoking furious bacchanales danced by whirling horrors in the unsoundable abysms of the Cosmos. Or again, in the loathsome depths of the crypt, on the bank of a subterranean and putrid river, the hero unwillingly participates in the celebration of an unholy cult, mingles with the worshippers who bow before a column of primordial fire before being taken away, astride those hybrid, winged, obscene monsters, toward the unhealthy darkness of a still deeper gulf. Beyond a blind wall or under the familiar pavement of streets, incommensurable abysms are opened for those who have heard the call. Space, suddenly, is decomposed. The familiar panorama of planes and axes around which Euclid of old organized space is dissolved.

48

The hero plunges into this chaos of forms, surfaces, and masses, falling at the same time into the foul and the unholy. But let the reader be reassured: Only the unfortunate, the unlucky, or the poor are—so Lovecraft says—exposed to these dangers. Only they who have nothing to lose could thus cross the futile setting that architects and town planners raise around us, to lose themselves, beyond those forbidden thresholds, amid unspeakable and demoniac marvels.

Sometimes space, instead of being circumscribed by the limits of a city, is unraveled and dilated, stretched and amplified infinitely, restricted only by the dreamer's imagination. As vast, multiformed, and colorful as diurnal space is dull and gray, it is, "beyond the wall of sleep," the place where every ecstasy and every liberty is realized. The images of motion thus depend on what Bachelard has nicely called the "poetics of wings": the dreamer seems to float in the air with ease and grace, moving about in an ethereal substance, flying over pleasant or sublime landscapes. Sometimes he moves as if swimming in unknown space, the internal arrangement of which corresponds to no familiar norm. Gilman, with preternatural ease, wanders among objects that have unexpected prismatic forms. The beings he meets resemble masses of compressed bubbles or undulating arabesques. He plunges into abysms of light and sound, crosses moving planes, geometrical forms with incomprehensible angles, iridescent bubbles, and multicolored polyhedrons. Sometimes his vision explodes in a gush of intimately mixed colors; then he finds himself on a high terrace overhanging a marvelous city, such as Dunsany never dreamed and Sime never drew, a city whose roofs, whose strangely formed domes, whose slender minarets are resplendent under the disconcerting splendor of a polychrome sky. . . .

This extreme expansion of space is for the dreamer a source of intense joy. In deep sleep, he wondrously realizes the perfect dynamism of flight from the constraints and heaviness of the flesh, beyond the easily reached limits of the diurnal world. With what enthusiasm these adventurers of dream move in the ether of infinite space, plunging toward vaporous abysms or, conversely, dashing in pursuit of some inaccessible star!

And yet, the dangers that lie in wait for them in the course of their great oneiric peregrinations are at once real and terrible. These boundless expanses they cross are as unstable as the images of a dream, and are populated by satanic presences. The darkest forces, the most terrible phantasms that preside over the activity of our profound psyche, have been driven back into dream, and move in our own inner space. No longer able, since the death of gods and devil, to inhabit the level of clear consciousness, they hide in our inner immensity and are only the more redoubtable there. There are, "beyond the wall of sleep," not only brothers of light who guide us toward ineffable splendors, but also the lurking enemy against whom we must fight in a battle whose dimensions have now become cosmic. Sometimes, at the depths of the gulfs over which the dreamer flies, the glimmers that are their eyes shine, the membranous wings that carry sinister messages rustle. Or again some superb and obsolete deity, irritated at the dreamer's audacity, stops him dead, nevermore to search in his quest: in the morning we find in an empty bed a petrified head, worthy of some ancient statuary . . .[7] or we find a corpse washed in his own blood: Brown Jenkin, the human rat, has devoured Gilman's heart, after having dug a channel through his body with teeth and claws.[8]

Space is a cruel place where it is in every way difficult to be. More than a place, it is an emanation of anguish, projecting itself in volumes, being propagated along axes and surfaces, crystallizing at privileged levels. The homes, the cities, the cellars, the Cosmos are perhaps less a setting where horror is actualized than where horror is made tangible and localized. All is fantasy—the gaping void where Carter plunges vertiginously after having leaped from the shantak as well as the subterranean sites where the characters are locked up. Open space and closed recesses, infinitely vast and minuscule—such are the conceptions of fear.

In Lovecraft, however, the space of fantasy is not to be confounded entirely with the space of dream. In this it differs from the marvelous and redoubtable gulfs imagined by Lord Dunsany, which have the fragility of our dreams. We walk there, and have strange encounters; but they vanish like soap bubbles in the sun as soon as we leave them. Pegāna has no other existence than in the dreams of Māna-Yood-Sushāī. For Lovecraft, however, dream is not contained in the Beyond, but gives access to it. On waking the horror remains: Gilman convulsively holds tight in his hand an objet d'art that, made of a metal unknown on earth, testifies to the material reality of the spaces he has visited.

The economy of the fantasy tale demands this realism. It is because the reader cannot reduce Gilman's adventures to the dimensions of a simple nightmare that the bizarre enters. The dreams, though strange, are restored to the familiar domain of science, and the statuette that links Gilman with his mad nocturnal escapades—or again the extraordinary jewelry preserved in the museum of Miskatonic University in Arkham—forms the proof of the impossible and suddenly opens whirling perspectives on the inconceivable.

Here a point must be made: Lovecraft's *realism* concerns his art and not, evidently, his thought. The existence of these faraway worlds, necessary though they may be to fantastic creation, is in his work in no way postulated as the object of a personal certitude. On the contrary, we have emphasized the radical skepticism of the author. In his tales he only plays with his fears and dreams, and also with the possibilities opened to the imagination by Einstein's theories on the space-time continuum. Lovecraft, lover of astronomy, had in 1923 enthusiastically discovered the theory of relativity, in which he thought he had found the justification for his absolute pessimism. He later made frequent allusions to it in his letters, in terms that let us suppose he had a precise enough understanding of these questions.[9] What a marvelous aid he found in the work of the great physicist, being thus able to give his imaginary fantasies, his "arabesques" and other "grotesque" themes, a scientific foundation! But at no moment does he believe, on the level of clear consciousness, in the physical reality of the spaces attained by his characters.

Still less does he adhere to the beliefs, or give himself up to the rituals, of any esoteric sect or secret society. The personality of a Lovecraft, such as is drawn from his letters, is very different from that, for example, of a Machen, who was affiliated with the Golden Dawn and doubtless not very far from believing in the theoretical possibility of manifestations of the Beyond. Lovecraft was an incorrigible skeptic from one end of his existence to the other, and his "materialistic monism" separated him from all adherence to such a body of mystical doctrine. The popular articles on the origin of life and the world, the ceaseless rumors transmitted by a type of press concerning eventual "invaders" or touching on the secret existence of "The Great Race," only turned him cold. We hope that Messrs. Pauwels and Bergier will forgive us:[10] *reality* was for him never fantastic; it was to escape reality that he created his impossible parallel universe. For him, the fantastic had to be, in artistry, a realistic fantastic. It is one thing to explore haunting regions in dream and to give them in a tale all the density and presence of reality; it is another to believe in the material existence of a Beyond, or more simply of an "Outside," absolute or not.

The creator of Randolph Carter surely did not believe in the existence of other worlds except those he visited in dream, and whose forms he substituted, by a gratuitous composition that is at the source of all art, for those of the diurnal world. This relates him much more to the *fantaisistes* of the past—the Gothic novelists and the Victorian writers—than to the believers of any esotericism. There is, however, this reserve: Lovecraft's Beyond is different from those imagined by Lewis, Maturin, Sheridan LeFanu, or Walter de la Mare. For these writers, the Beyond lacks dimension; it is an undetermined place, without mass or thickness, whose function is limited: it suffices to house the inadmissible for the duration of the tale, to lodge that which by its very nature can exist only outside a rational framework. For Lovecraft, the Beyond is not a simple *alibi;* it is a space that, though situated on the other side of the world, has a length, width, and, above all, a *depth.* It has the dimensions of our inner universe. It too is perpetually mobile and in continuous extension; it too is strictly dependent on time. It contracts and dilates, stretches and deepens to the rhythm of the pulsations of our psyche.

Lovecraft's tales are, in a way, only a vast attempt at the dramatization of space, rendered agonizing by his dynamics, and fantastic insofar as its unforeseeable metamorphoses come to trouble the Euclidean order of things. Under the cover of the theory of relativity, the author's purpose remains clear: he wishes to disquiet his too wise and too perfectly integrated contemporaries, communicating to them his fear, hurling them from their lethargic assurance, making them aware that they are only a moment away from the abysms of horror that threaten to open suddenly under their feet. The known world, the universe of the charts and maps, is but a negligible part of "total reality," of that space-time continuum Einstein alone perceived. Familiar space where we lead our narrow existence is a ridiculous space of merely three dimensions. On the other side of the Ultimate Gate, which cannot be opened but by the Silver Key, Randolph Carter finally learns the truth: the world is not *made* from the simplest geometric forms, but is *inferred* from infinitely complex forms, superimposed in a pyramidal and infinite hierarchy. Each figure of two dimensions, he is told, is formed by the intersection of a plane and a mass, that is, that

which corresponds to a cut made from a figure of one more dimension. Thus the square exists from the cube and the circle from the
sphere. But the cube and the sphere are also formed by the intersection of a mass of three dimensions and a figure of one more
dimension, these figures being in turn cut from forms of five dimensions, and so on "up to the dizzy and reachless heights of
archetypal infinity."[11] The result is that what we take for reality is
but a ridiculous illusion. We are in constant touch with worlds
encased each in the other, multiplying to infinity; we too run the
risk of falling into these complicated spaces that broaden the field
of action of the characters beyond the possible or the imaginable.

To make man more ludicrous, Lovecraft places him in a "plu-
rality of worlds" that contemporary scientific theories confirm. But
let us not be fooled: the laws that preside over the metamorphoses
of space in his tales are not the ones that arise from strict principles. The references to Einstein are there merely to justify crudely
and superficially an action whose purpose is the hazardous, hesi-
tant exploration of the utter depths of the psyche. The reader must
feel disoriented, lost, and powerless, and what better way to reach
this end than to make him enter the thousand and one labyrinths
of a delirium . . . knowingly controlled?

Only when the familiar setting collapses can the fantastic adventure begin.

THE HORRIFIC BESTIARY

Thus horror alone is left me as my peculiar kingdom, and in it I must hold my lowly reproduction of a Plutonian court.
—Lovecraft[1]

To enter Lovecraft's fantastic universe is to be brutally dislodged from the familiar, dispossessed of all criteria or systems of reference, violently thrown into an abnormal space amid beings of which the least one can say is that they transgress the common order. The monster plays no negligible role in this basic bewilderment; it surprises, it frightens, it shocks. To be sure, it long ago acquired the right of being summoned in art and literature. But the multiheaded gargoyles of the cathedrals, as well as the devils and damned beings of Bosch, are not truly fantastic, for they merely illustrate a moral discourse and are the adjuncts of a popular catechism. The fabulous beings of classical mythology are too allegorical to inspire real terror. Such, moreover, is not their aim.

Abstract and immobile, their primary function is in primitively recounting the world.

This is not the place for a debate on teratology. It is, however, useful to say that a monster is not *by nature* fantastic. It becomes truly so only if it manifests itself outside all systems and all doctrines. Animated with a perverse autonomy, it must assert itself in its total freedom. Nothing or no one ought to be able to explain it away, or to integrate it into a theology or a cosmogony. Historically, the first authentically fantastic monsters date from the beginning of the nineteenth century, that is, from the moment fable was divorced from belief. But although in the Romantic era, fond as it was of excess, the monstrous was only too often the rusty machinery of horror, there is at the source of the extraordinary creatures invented by Lovecraft a dynamism of imagination, which gives them a profound and redoubtable originality. After meeting them but once, we can hardly forget these hideous beings who in one long, unbelievable procession cross the landscape of New England; they are carriers of vital images that help define the author's personal myth. And clearly the radical skepticism we have emphasized in him, the independence of this dreamer from churches and philosophies and sects, is not unrelated to this perfect success.

More often, Lovecraft's monsters do not stray radically from the human form. They keep its general aspect, its silhouette, but are endowed at the same time with attributes that belong to a different animal species. They are characterized above all by their *hybridism* —a hybridism that is not the simple juxtaposition of disparate elements as in some monsters of antiquity, but a result of a sort of contamination or collective pollution.

The Deep Ones, for example, have kept many aspects of their original humanity, even when strolling through the streets of shadowed Innsmouth with the waddling gait of batrachians. We do not wish to speak of the black frock coats and striped trousers with which they cover themselves to hide the shining and viscous skin of their white bellies, nor of the hats with which they grotesquely dress their fishlike heads, the protruding eyes of which are always open. Despite their webbed feet and their gills, despite the croaks and yelps, which for them now replace language, there is in them something that pathetically recalls the men they once were. The context induces us to think that they are the fruits of unclean weddings between marine monstrosities and the young girls of the town, thus representing the outcome of a slow degeneration. The entire community of Innsmouth was soiled from the moment Captain Obed Marsh brought in his strange secrets from faraway islands. The relative humanity of the Deep Ones, that is to say, their still detectable relation to the human species, is the very source of the anguish that grips the narrator of "The Shadow over Innsmouth." He is disquieted, and rightly so, by the imprecise menace created by the atrocious metamorphosis undergone by people like himself. The end of the tale is, as we will see, significant in this respect. The monster is revolting not only because it escapes logic and constitutes a disturbance for the reason, but also because it is propagated and, little by little, corrupts the individuals of a healthy race. In a land of fantasy no one can be certain—and the reader least of all—that he will not someday be changed into a monster.

The demoniac beasts of "The Lurking Fear" have a similar origin. Here again we are disconcerted by the inconceivable: That swarming and nauseous wave of deformed and diabolically inimical creatures who mate and devour one another in the cellars and subterranean corridors of the old house of Martense is enough of a surprise. But the true horror is aroused by the still human appearance of these whitish, yellow-fanged apes who are the frightful result of repeated consanguinous unions and the ultimate stage of degeneracy of a once flourishing family.[2] The hideous multiplying of these monsters illustrates in a particularly adequate way one of Lovecraft's major obsessions: sexuality carries in it a fatal germ of corruption and the profanation of the race. The many degenerates who populate the backward region of the Catskills where the drama unfolds are also there to testify to this.

It is not by chance, it seems, that the particularly repulsive region of Massachusetts that serves as the setting for "The Dunwich Horror" also contains many simpletons and half-wits.[3] The presence of the strange or abnormal is not manifested only by the blighting of the landscape, but also by the withering of intellects. Here also there has been a transgression of the principle of segregation among species: Wilbur is born after unheard-of, unimaginable sexual rapports between Yog-Sothoth—that abominable deity from the stars—and a slightly retarded farm girl. This double heredity of character is, moreover, physically perceptible. From his mother he holds a roughly human outline: a thick face with receding chin and the hands of a peasant. To his extraterrestrial father he owes his fabulous monstrosities, all localized in the lower parts of his body:

> Below the waist, though, it was the worst; for here all human re-semblances left off and sheer phantasy began. The skin was thickly covered with coarse black fur, and from the abdomen a score of long greenish-grey tentacles with red sucking mouths protruded limply. Their arrangement was odd, and seemed to follow the symmetries of some cosmic geometry unknown to earth or the solar system. On each of the hips, deep set in a kind of pinkish, ciliated orbit, was what seemed to be a rudimentary eye; whilst in lieu of a tail there depended a kind of trunk or feeler with purple annular markings, and with many evidences of being an undeveloped mouth or throat. The limbs, save for their black fur, roughly resembled the hind legs of prehistoric earth's giant saurians; and terminated in ridgy-veined pads that were neither hooves nor claws. When the thing breathed, its tail and tentacles rhythmically changed colour, as if from some circulatory cause normal to the non-human side of its ancestry. In the tentacles this was observable as a deepening of the greenish tinge, whilst in the tail it was manifest as a yellowish appearance which alternated with a sickly greyish-white in the spaces between the purple rings.[4]

Such are the beings we encounter in the Lovecraftian universe: monsters that under their clothing hide singular anomalies and are all the more dangerous because they come and go amid men without usually being bothered. But what is even more serious is that Wilbur has a twin brother who is totally invisible. We can only guess his inconceivable dimensions by the traces of desolation and death that he leaves in his wake. The peasants, dismayed at the sight of round footprints "as big as barrel-heads,"[5] imagined that the monster was something like an elephant. There were, however, more prints than could have been made by a four-pawed animal. . . . Some attributed to him the size of a moving house or mountain. And when the rational professors who swore to exterminate the thing made it visible for an instant by a device they had invented, the spectacle offered to the eyes of the witnesses was not a little revolting.

And yet, the invisible monster differed from his brother Wilbur only in that he had received a greater part of what Lovecraft calls "outsideness." Only the half-face, which surmounted this formless and swarming mass of gelatinous tentacles, revealed the part inherited from the human species. Without the courage and the science of a handful of men, the prophecy of the mad Arab Abdul Alhazred, recorded in the hideous *Necronomicon*, would have been realized and the earth would have known the coming of one who is the gate, the key, and the guardian of the gate. After summer comes winter; after winter, spring. Iä! Shub-Niggurath!

There are many other monsters in the Lovecraftian universe. Indeed, there is not a tale where they do not intervene in some manner or other. Randolph Carter, on the road to marvelous Kadath, meets more than one. In the Land of Deeper Slumber, which he has reached after having descended the seven hundred steps of dream, many suspicious forms roam. The night-gaunts with their cold, humid, and viscous bodies, their bat-wings, their prehensile claws, and particularly *their total absence of face* are at least as repulsive as the Deep Ones. The same holds for the "blasphemous lunar entities," flabby, gelatinous, and whitish, whose toadlike bodies stretch and contract at will and who when pierced spew an intolerable stench. Nor are the gugs very reassuring: nearly seven yards tall, they are vaguely anthropomorphic, with a grotesque barrel-like head whose mouth opens *vertically*, splitting the face from bottom to top. And we need not speak of the shantaks, those flying, hippocephalic, and shell-covered elephants, nor of the repugnant ghasts.

If in the depths of dream one can conceivably deal with these demons, as is testified by some of Carter's alliances with the ghouls and the night-gaunts, on the surface it is entirely otherwise: the monsters of the Waking World are always satanic, aggressive, animated by perverse intentions. Without pretending to list them all, we must again cite the pinkish, crustacean-bodied, ellipsoid-headed beings,[6] come from the planet Yuggoth,[7] who in "The Whisperer in Darkness" scatter fright among the hill-dwellers of Vermont. We must also note the indefinite, gelatinous, and perpetually swarming monstrosities that Tillinghast, in "From Beyond," succeeds at the price of his life in making appear for an instant. We must particularly speak of the ghouls and vampires who populate so many of the "diurnal" tales, these cousins whom Dracula himself would surely have hesitated to meet: the one in "The Shunned House," with a vague and gigantic form,[8] or the incredible "outsider," who emerges from the deepest layers of dream and whose physical aspect is literally delirious.[9]

But we have not finished naming or describing these nightmarish creatures. Yet it is less important to accumulate horrible details than to try to understand them. From the start we will make this assertion: the Lovecraftian monster—in any case the one manifesting itself in the harsh light of the Waking World—is less frightening than . . . repugnant. His attributes seem singularly vivid. He is characterized in a specific fashion by his *viscosity* (he is gummy, sticky, and on occasion secretes greenish humors), his *inconsistency* (he is soft, flabby, gelatinous), the intense *stench* that he releases (fetid exhalations or the strong odor of fish), and his swarming *multiplicity,* composed as he often is of an infinity of globulous corpuscles (we think of that "shapeless congeries of protoplasmic bubbles, faintly self-luminous, and with myriads of temporary eyes forming and unforming as pustules of greenish light" in *At the Mountains of Madness*[10]) or of membranous tentacles animated with a perpetual and sickening agitation (the twin brother of Wilbur Whateley is in all our memories . . .).

The Lovecraftian monster is doubtless blindly cruel and devastating; the list in each tale is long of the victims whom he massacres or maims. The extreme panic, however, that seizes the characters is less explained by their fear of death than by their instinctive refusal of all contact with the monster. It is much more terrible to see it, to sense it, to smell it—*touching* it being at any rate out of the question—than actually to face death. Lovecraft's tales are full of these great traumatics who, one day confronted with the Abominable, henceforth drag out miserable lives, which even drugs do not make endurable. The monster, before being the source of terror, is initially the focus of all distaste.

Need we suggest that the crystallization of such repulsions is the pathognomonic sign of profound, manifest lesions? Without pretending to enter into a detailed discussion of matters about which we are admittedly ill-prepared, we can at least venture to suppose that a being like Wilbur, whose monstrousness is localized *below the waist,* is a carrier of very precise meanings. A psychoanalyst would clearly have much to say about these anomalies. The Lovecraftian monsters are certainly no longer the allegories of an ancient world (the centaur was a man in the upper portions, animal and not *monster* below), nor the decorative elements of a baroque facade. The Deep Ones and the ghouls are not monsters of the surface, nor the blithe compositions of a jeu d'esprit; they surge, surely unbeknown to their creator, from the darkest zones of the psyche, and it is precisely their reaching the level of the diurnal world that makes them what they are. Insofar as they remain hidden in the depths of dream, they move in a strange enough universe, but one where their monstrousness remains hazy and indefinite. In his subterranean castle, the unclean loner of "The Outsider" lacks the ability to identify himself. He truly becomes a monster, or recognizes himself as such, only when he sees himself in a mirror or meets human eyes. These unnameable creatures, on which are fixed all the repugnances and anguish of the author, emerge from this underside of life, and only a professional analyst should legitimately sound their depths.

As for us, being unable to make a serious opinion on the pathological origin of these monsters, we may as well orient our analysis toward other realities. Would it be truly wrong to make note, in connection with these fundamentally hybrid and repugnant entities that populate Lovecraft's tales, of other "monsters" that the author describes in his letters and that seem to have inspired in him as intense a repulsion? We think of those strangers, those "foreigners" of every shade and hue who teem unbearably in the slums of New York and to whom Lovecraft gives, when he speaks of them, the same attributes as the Deep Ones or the infamous progeny of Yog-Sothoth: a swarming nature, an uncertain consistency, a stench, a gelatinous quivering, and so on. It seems significant that nearly the same terms are used to describe, for example, the descendants of the Martenses in "The Lurking Fear" and the "Italo-Semitico-Mongoloids" who filter and ooze in the street from the windows and doors of their dens, recalling "the swarming of worms in the carcass" or the "unpleasant entities of the deep sea."[11]

Singular analogies seem to be established between the foreigner and the monster, between the immigrant Kurd or Chinese and the "outsider." For Lovecraft, fond as we have proven of pure blood— this Viking proud of his Aryan ancestry—the displaying of these execrable mutants seems perhaps, in an obscure and confusing way, a testimonial to the failure of America's politics of racial assimilation, a deliberate rejection of the notion of the "melting pot," which forms so integral a part of the American dream. In this man, ever faithful to the ideologies of the past, any infringement of the strictest segregation ends in disastrous, in *monstrous*, consequences. It is perhaps this he wishes to suggest when he makes note of the retarded mentalities of peasants, mountain-dwellers, and city-dwellers (these last being mainly Italians, Poles, or Orientals) around each zone of horror, or wherever the monstrous is manifested. Thus the monsters, fruit of repugnant matings of humans with "outsiders," represent the ultimate level of degeneracy that lies in wait for American civilization if it continues to encourage, or simply to tolerate, the mixture of bloods and races; hybridism, cross-breeding are at the source of the monstrous.

And because we have here taken up the game of hypothesis and conjecture, let us have the audacity not to stop half way. We would like to use a particularly horrible tale to illustrate our thesis. If in "Herbert West—Reanimator" it is no longer a question of monsters engendered by unheard-of sexual rapports, the philosophy of the tale seems to us not any less troubling. Do these "composite entities" Dr. West makes from anatomical elements, taken here and there from the cemeteries of the city, have only a purely anecdotal significance? We willingly confess that they raise disconcerting echoes in us, particularly when at the end of the tale these disparately membered monsters, made of bits and pieces, avenge themselves cruelly on their imprudent sire. America, the author seems to want to tell us through his own phantasms, may one day also regret having spawned its monsters.

Thus, without prejudging ulterior, complementary, or contradictory interpretations, it seems legitimate to invest the Lovecraftian monster with a political significance, in the sense that it is developed on a level of consciousness that is at the moment difficult to specify, but one that remains always in strict dependence on the author's racial and fascistic theories. The monster does not have his origin only in pathological behavior; it is also the projection, in the black chamber of a sick mind, of the hate and disgust felt for the stranger, the outsider, whose presence at the heart of American civilization is a stain and a menace of corruption.

5

THE DEPTHS OF HORROR

> Who can, with my knowledge, think of the earth's unknown caverns without a nightmare dread of future possibilities? I cannot see a well or a subway entrance without shuddering.
>
> —"The Lurking Fear"[1]

Although in other fantasy writers the domain of the Beyond is difficult to locate precisely, it is easy to show that in Lovecraft it is almost always situated *in the depths*. In his tales it is no longer the convenient abstraction conceived by his predecessors to house the irrational, but a place situated under the reassuring surface of things, downward from "the edge of the world." The Inadmissible, which is also the Abominable—the equation is in itself full of meaning—is hidden in the utter depths of the subsoil. The Impossible, which is the Evil, gnaws secretly at the very foundation of American civilization. Dark and harmful forces, born of the underside of the world, threaten at any moment to break out upon the Waking World.

The irrational in Lovecraft's tales seems indissociable from the images of the depths. The abnormal, the disquieting, and the unclean are, on the vertical axis of the imagination, always situated toward the bottom, in the zone of the deepest shade. In the house, which according to Bachelard represents one of the "symbols of our consciousness of verticality,"[2] one of the "vertical schemas of human psychology,"[3] horror is always buried in the cellar. The house is, par excellence, the place where everything that escapes from conscious control is performed. In the Lovecraftian topography it represents the privileged place where the reassuring images of the surface are most easily and most totally transformed into dream. In contrast with the attic, which is the place of sublimation, the cellar is the place of horror. "But after all," writes the narrator of "The Shunned House," "the attic was not the most terrible part of the house. It was the dank, humid cellar which somehow exerted the strongest repulsion on us. . . ."[4]

There are, however, in some of Lovecraft's tales examples of elevated places associated with terror. In "The Dreams in the Witch House" the Inconceivable is manifested in the highest story of the house, in the mansard room where Gilman lives and dreams. In "The Strange High House in the Mist" it seems that fear, as if suspended in the sky, has settled at the very summit of the high crags that surround Kingsport, the "archaic" city.[5] In "The Haunter of the Dark" the abominable "entity" that menaces the city of Providence and the world is entirely hidden in the top of a church steeple.

But if we look at them more closely, we notice that in the first of these three tales, the disposition of the walls and ceiling—which obey no principle of Euclidean geometry—permits a young student of mathematics to escape by night toward other, cosmic depths; the deep can, we will see, sometimes be situated above. Analogously, in the second tale—manifestly written under the patronage of Dunsany—the opaque and sealed windows of the house of the Terrible Old Man do not give out on to the world, but the Cosmos, that is, a reversed abysm. In the third tale, the interior of the steeple, totally hidden by night, *simulates* a depth, a dream site, by the very darkness in which it is perpetually plunged. Light, an essential attribute of upper spheres, prohibits Nyarlathotep, the

"Dark God," from manifesting himself; thus is it rigorously, if artificially (remember that electrical breakdown), banished. Except for these tales, and perhaps some other less important ones, it is striking to observe that in Lovecraft horror always comes from below. All these old colonial homes of which Lovecraft was passionately fond are drawn on his imaginary map only to signal the location of great depths. It is there that dream-space is dug, stretching infinitely toward the bottom, pushing its roots across the opaque thickness of the soil; to cite Bachelard again, "terror yields us to the earth."[6]

For example, that old, dilapidated hovel rented by Pickman in hoary Boston, where the homes seem not to have been constructed by men's hands but to have come out of the earth like dubious plants, is one of the privileged sites where the secret horror from the cellar emerges. By a complicated system of underground labyrinths and mysterious routes that end at the basement of this century-abandoned dwelling, there emerges into the world all that the lower darkness calls the most horrible, the most unbelievable, the most repugnant: vaguely bipedal forms of canine physiognomy, who fill their bellies amply at the neighboring cemetery before dashing off on their interminable subterranean peregrinations, and whom the painter photographs to represent them later, with refreshed mind, on his canvases. Thus, respectable Boston, with its picturesque streets and its old homes, is built on a gigantic molehill whose sinuous conduits are perpetually filled with a swarming and infamous life.

Similar things take place in New York. When Malone, the policeman in "The Horror at Red Hook," carries out his inquiry into that deadly zone of the city where thick-lipped Orientals abduct little blue-eyed Norwegian infants, there are discoveries in the cellar of a house near the harbor, which cause serious injury to his mental equilibrium. Having broken into a worm-eaten door, he is sucked into indescribable lower regions, plunging into a thick darkness peopled by demoniac presences:

> Avenues of limitless night seemed to radiate in every direction, till one might fancy that here lay the root of a contagion destined to sicken and swallow cities, and engulf nations in the foetor of hybrid pestilence. Here cosmic sin had entered, and festered by unhallowed rites had commenced the grinning march of death that was

to rot us all to fungous abnormalities too hideous for the grave's holding. Satan here held his Babylonish court, and in the blood of stainless childhood the leprous limbs of phosphorescent Lilith were laved. Incubi and succubae howled praise to Hecate, and headless moon-calves bleated to the Magna Mater. Goats leaped to the sound of thin accursed flutes, and Aegipans chased endlessly after misshapen fauns over rocks twisted like swollen toads. Moloch and Ashtaroth were not absent; for in this quintessence of all damnation the bounds of consciousness were let down, and man's fancy lay open to vistas of every realm of horror and every forbidden dimension that evil had power to mould.[7]

By these "unsealed wells of night"[8] there emerge to the surface the most archaic and therefore the most redoubtable deities who have ever presided over human destiny. It is the Kurds, we note, those foreigners with repugnant faces, who by their impious cults have revived certain sleeping forces of evil. Clandestinely installed amid garbage and stench, in one of the many areas where no efficacious police control is possible, they support this secret horror, which, by slow internal corruption, insidiously undermines the foundation of the most prestigious city in the United States. Under the skyscrapers of New York, these subterranean avenues branch out, opening on infamous cesspools, flowing into black and putrid rivers where primordial horrors swim.

In "The Festival" the narrator reaches these infernal sites after a prodigious descent along a spiral staircase cut into the rock, down to the "shaft of nighted mystery" where lateral tunnels issuing from "unknown recesses of blackness" converge. He learns that he is under the very soil of the city of Kingsport, and shivers at the idea "that a town should be so aged and maggoty with subterranean evil."[9]

Kingsport, New York, Boston: so many points on the map of the United States where a deep, contagious evil emerges to menace the peace of the world. But horror is not limited to the cities of the New World; it is manifested equally well, perhaps better, in countries with an old culture and a secular tradition. The subsoil of old England conceals comparable horrors. In a deep crypt in Exham Priory, with walls covered with alarming inscriptions for those versed in Latin, Walter de la Poer and his companions discover an altar whose slabs hide the entrance of a spiral staircase leading toward other depths: in the topography of dream, there is always a deeper level than that at which the actors of the dream find themselves. One significant and particularly disquieting detail is that the staircase seems to have been dug *from bottom to top,* as if to allow nameless beings installed in the ultradepths to emerge to the surface. The beckoning, the initiative, the call come from below, just as in "The Horror at Red Hook," where the door by which Malone descends into the underworld of Brooklyn splinters less under the effect of a push than of a suction exerted from below.

In "The Rats in the Walls," as elsewhere, all descent is descent toward the irrational, the unclean, the blasphemous. These cultured and skeptical characters must surrender to the evidence: in a gigantic grotto all around them, edifices and tumuli are raised whose style attests to their prodigious age, while their feet tread on piled-up remnants of hideous feasts and visible signs of sacrilegious rituals. We need say nothing yet about de la Poer's behavior when the exact nature of his ancestors' crime is suddenly revealed to him; let us reserve that for later. For the present we will show once again that a secret and ancient evil menaces the most prestigious families from within, an evil born of the most archaic layers of the collective unconscious.

We could illustrate this basic obsession of the author by many other examples; but let it suffice to remember that in "The Lurking Fear" it is in the underground tunnels of an old colonial home that the frightful descendants of Martense hid once their degeneration began; or that in "The Shunned House" the vampire is buried in the ground of the cellar; or that in "The Shadow over Innsmouth" the focus of horror is in a marine gulf some distance from the port: the sea, insofar as it is a primordial, mythical element, is particularly adapted for concealing horror. It is, let us not forget, at the very bottom of the ocean that, in an engulfed temple, there reposes—but for how much longer?—the god Cthulhu.

A quintessential leprosy gnaws at the underside of the world, placed in the very heart of things—such is the demon Azathoth in his Ultimate Abyss. It is worth noting that time, like space, is contaminated. This is to say that horror is housed in the utter depths of the past just as it is in the utter depths of the earth. The descent to ultradeep sites coincides always with a regression to an anterior stage of chronology. In "The Shunned House" the narrator must explore the local past of Providence at the same time that he, in the cellar of his uncle's home, gives way to those experiences we know only too well. In "The Rats in the Walls," analogously, de la Poer and his friends descend the steps of that infernal spiral staircase and so plunge progressively and by stages into a past, into the ultimate history of a family and . . . into evil.

The more the past is hidden (the Kurds who aid the sinister Suydam in his forbidden researches are the descendants of the Yezidis, Satan-worshippers from the beginning of time) the more it resembles myth and tends to be confounded with it, thus lending itself better to fable. Time is another abysm into which we might very possibly fall. And we never know at the start how long the fall will last. The characters may find themselves in some distant yet always historical epoch, as with Peaslee amid the "Great Race," who lived on the earth 150 million years before our era and some of whom are "as old as the Cosmos."

No one takes this professor seriously—and his colleagues at the celebrated Miskatonic University at Arkham least of all—when he tries timidly to explain what has happened to him. When, however, he finds in an Australian desert what he believes to be the site of his past adventures, there begins the most fabulous expedition ever undertaken by man, in search of his own origins. He slides between Cyclopean blocks of rock, follows tunnels manifestly dug by other tools than those puny ones used by humans, and plunges dangerously into a black abysm which forges the opaque blackness of elapsed time: significantly, the images of the depths are attached to history, for they are tied to the earth. As he descends and knocks against walls, doors, and labyrinths, he orients himself not by the pale beam of his torch but by the vivid memories they stir in him. But once grasping the proof of the inadmissible—when, in those records infinitely older than the human species, he recognizes his own handwriting—he slides and falls into new abysms, toward primordial horrors:

> There was a hideous fall through incalculable leagues of viscous, sentient darkness, and a babel of noises utterly alien to all that we know of the earth and its organic life. Dormant, rudimentary senses seemed to start into vitality within me, telling of pits and voids peopled by floating horrors and leading to sunless crags and oceans and teeming cities of windowless, basalt towers upon which no light ever shone.
>
> Secrets of the primal planet and its immemorial aeons flashed through my brain without the aid of sight or sound, and there were known to me things which not even the wildest of former dreams had ever suggested. And all the while cold fingers of damp vapour clutched and picked at me, and that eldritch, damnable whistling

shrieked fiendishly above all the alternations of babel and silence in the whirlpools of darkness around.[10]

However far Peaslee was from the level of the surface, he had to undergo yet again the experience of the fall—how characteristic a dream-experience!—and descend lower, always lower, to meet horror at the bottom of the gulf, at the bottom of time.[11]

Lovecraft was decidedly fascinated with the sciences that allowed the investigation of the earliest stretches of time. His scholars are ethnologists, folklorists, and geologists. In *At the Mountains of Madness* the narrator organizes a scientific expedition to the Antarctic (the author owed this to Poe)[12] whose goal is the study of deep-buried rock. In the course of these researches the scientists one day encounter, in the debris of primitive shellfish and fragments of divers bones of archaic mammals, the monstrous fossils of organisms several thousand million years old. In the Lovecraftian universe there is manifestly an "edge of time" as well as an "edge of the world," and the author, close to vertigo, ill resists the attraction of this new gulf.

In attaining this anterior period in history, Lovecraft was as always aided by antique homes and cities, whose architectural structures guide the imagination in its dynamic descent. The depths of space they define, around the vertical axis of their spiral staircase, are an adequate materialization of the shadows out of time that seem to have hypnotized the author. Here again the exploration of a mythic past coincides with the descent of two survivors of the expedition along subterranean tunnels and helicoidal inclined planes, in the ruins of the ancient city that still remain on the deserted and inaccessible expanse of the malefic Plateau of Leng. The frescoes they admire as they plunge into the nighted gulf record the history of those who once lived there, thus creating a type of inverse chronology. The metamorphosis of the universe at the heart of geological cycles and the stages of the fabulous existence of the Old Ones unravel thus *backward* before our eyes.

The descent into the entrails of the earth corresponds to a voyage in time. For then, at the bottom of the abyss and at the end of their quest, the adventurers encounter a . . . shoggoth, still living, a plastic and globulous entity, which by suction decapitates the last descendants of a prestigious race. The whole tale aims once more at this reactivation of a latent horror, which lies, always menacing, beyond space and time, at the heart of the world. "It is absolutely necessary, for the peace and safety of mankind, that some of earth's dark, dead corners and unplumbed depths be let alone; lest sleeping abnormalities wake to resurgent life, and blasphemously surviving nightmares squirm and splash out of their black lairs to newer and wider conquests."[13]

It is within the framework of these remarks on the images of the deep—characteristic, we think, of his writing—that it is useful to read Lovecraft's pseudo–science fiction tales. There is sometimes a tendency to class some of his tales ("The Colour out of Space," for example, or "The Whisperer in Darkness") as among the masterpieces of that other and similar genre. This assimilation, however, can seem wrong if we consider that interstellar space is perceived by our author less as the exciting place of future adventures than as a type of reversed abysm, another depth at the other extremity of the vertical axis of the imagination, an "anti-gulf" from which new horrors come, always associated with the origins of the universe and not with its final ends. Lovecraft belongs to that class of dreamers for whom the deep is *also* above.

Is it not significant, moreover, that the horror out of space is buried immediately in the depths of the earth? It is at the bottom of a well on a farm that this malign, impalpable, immaterial presence from the stars is manifested. In this damned zone, corruption is brought up through the soil, comes up through the roots; vegetation rots, animals fall to dust, men crumble underfoot before dying. All life is sucked into the depths to nourish this vaporous monster, this atrocious, iridescent mist, which, having regained its strength, can thus reattain its original depths.

We find in "The Whisperer in Darkness" the same coming-and-going between two gulfs. Having come from the faraway planet Yuggoth, that strange globe situated "at the rim of the solar system,"[14] the crustacean-bodied monsters have from the fabulous times of Cthulhu founded a secret colony on earth. Coming from the hidden abysms of the Cosmos, their first concern was to attain the secret depths of the earth. By these unknown entrances, they have penetrated to the heart of our planet and rediscovered the swarming world of life in the kingdoms of K'n-yan, Yoth, and N'kai. . . . It is from this subterranean base that they have, from time immemorial, inflicted upon men the abominable experiences that we know but too well. The great terror that rises from the earth had first fallen from the stars.

Perhaps we are now in a better position to define the substance of Lovecraft's fantastic creation. It is, to be sure, firstly a matter of an "art of causing fear,"[15] seeking to dissipate the anesthetic effects of modern society, hyperrational and reassuring. Doubtless there is also in his tales, conforming with the most modern definitions of the genre, the irruption of the inadmissible, the intolerable, into a world otherwise harmonious, "where the laws of nature," as Caillois has written, "are held to be inflexible and immutable." But Lovecraft, entirely respecting the rules of the game, proceeds in a manner peculiar to him: he creates the strange, he excites fear, by *turning the world inside out*. For Lovecraft, writing is the making of the oneiric and wrong side of things appear, substituting the nocturnal for the diurnal, replacing the reassuring image of the Waking World by the alienating ones of the great depths. The world of the surface has in his work no other raison d'être than provisionally and imperfectly to cover up the abyss. It has reality only insofar as it is in danger of being invaded by a wave of swarming horrors temporarily lulled, which the least imprudence could reactivate. All these pits, all these traps, all these shafts, which open under the feet of his heroes, are so many privileged points where the monsters of the great depths appear, or threaten to appear.

These images hold a signification. The endless steps, the inclined planes, the spirals that bore into space lead no doubt to the elements of a setting, but as surely perhaps to the obscurest region of abysmal life. The vertical axis that they define forms an inner place, a space inside which the author, more than his characters, explores his dreams with muffled and agonized steps. Are the monsters that populate his oeuvre perhaps those he discovers, or imagines he discovers, in the very depths of himself? We think of the slabs, the heavy rocks that the actors of certain dramas cautiously place over the orifices of the lower world: a wise measure taken by *those who know* to maintain their demons in a thankful lethargy. . . . But it is a tenacious evil, inscribed in the obscurest folds of the past, and it laughs at such obstacles, breaks all the barriers, and is perpetuated from age to age. . . .

6

THE HORRORS OF HEREDITY

You know Pickman comes of old Salem stock, and had a witch ancestor hanged in 1692.

—"Pickman's Model"[1]

Installed at the heart of the world and corrupting it from within, the monster is there, thick, hideous, aggressive, terrifying to the soul and physically dangerous.

Whence does it come? *Unde hoc monstrum?* It is not enough to say that it is hidden in the depths of the American soil, ready to transform "colonial New England into a kind of annex of hell,"[2] or to emerge from the course of millennia and surge to the surface of the present. Such a localization would be in a sense reassuring, for it would permit the characters to escape without too much difficulty from the effects of an evil that would be somewhat exterior. Actually, the depths of time and the earth where these malefic forces sleep are also *our* depths. Lovecraft's supreme skill consists in studying and presenting to the reader the progressive but ineluctable transformation of the monster-object into the monster-subject. In some particularly successful tales the monster is not the "pure someone else" of which Vax speaks; he becomes "I." But is this skill? Or was Lovecraft trying to free himself by speaking of one of his major obsessions? We must decide later.

Evil is in us. Let us certainly not imagine that the author was donning the robe of the theologian: Lovecraft is not St. Augustine. All the characters are, in the proper sense, potential monsters. In those tales where a being around whom the reader has identified himself is metamorphosed into a hideous or repulsive creature, the author—voluntarily or not—gains the better of himself. In suddenly shattering the last link that still unites his oeuvre with reality, or rather in showing us that reason carries in itself its own germ of corruption, he abolishes all absolutes, all certitude, all systems of reference. The reader is left adrift, *disoriented* in the most material sense of the term. Amid the multiple constituents that make up the impossible definition of the fantastic event, nothing is, we believe, more basic than this ultimate questioning of what has so long remained uncontested: the adherence of the narrator, the "witness," to the norm.

It is by heredity that the monstrous acts. We thus understand the importance of the genealogical researches in which so many of the characters are engaged. The metamorphosis that takes place in them most often has its origins in the fascination an ancestor exerts upon them. The corruption enveloping them surges from the recesses of their familial history. Precisely like the vegetation in "The Lurking Fear" and "The Colour out of Space," their genealogical tree is attacked through the roots.

In "The Shadow over Innsmouth" it all begins when the young narrator decides to spend most of his vacation in touring New England—for "sightseeing, antiquarian, and genealogical"[3] ends—and it is on the road from Arkham, cradle of his mother's family, that he finds adventure. As for Charles Dexter Ward, he only begins his researches, which will lead him to that abominable end which we all know, after discovering that he is descended from Joseph Curwen. "That he at once took an interest in everything pertaining to the bygone mystery is not to be wondered at; for every vague rumour that he had heard of Curwen now became something vital to himself, in whom flowed Curwen's blood. No spirited and imaginative genealogist could have done otherwise than begin forthwith an avid and systematic collection of Curwen data."[4]

This obsession with a vampiric heredity sucking on the hero's personality from within emerged very early in Lovecraft's work, for we find its traces in one of his earliest tales, "The Tomb." In Jervas Dudley there is already everything that for Lovecraft characterizes the *descendant:* an exceptional susceptibility to dream, a pronounced taste for old books, and a fascination for tombs. He knows not, when he spends entire nights in the empty coffin of his ancestor Hyde, that he obeys impulses originating from a dubious zone of his own line. Nor does he know, when becoming *the other,* speaking in archaic language and adopting manners not of his era, that he is truly possessed. Would it perhaps be more accurate to say that he is *dispossessed* of his body by a malefic will of his own blood? Certainly Jervas passes for a lunatic; and he is, no doubt, but in a far graver sense than his family and friends suspect. . . . According to Lovecraft, alienation is a phenomenon born of the depths of atavism.

"The Festival" illustrates this call of ancestry in a slightly different way. To respond to the summoning of distant relatives the narrator betakes himself to Kingsport, city of the dead. This invitation, by which he, along with others of his clan, is made to participate in a sacrilegious cult celebrated on Christmas day, forms a new proof of the vigilance of the departed. How can we rejoin them, if not by ourselves passing through the tomb, the yawning vault in the nave of the church that leads to secret crypts and to the depths of the familial past?

But although in "The Festival" the anonymous narrator by all his strength refuses to commune with the abominable mysteries offered him by his own people, in "The Shadow over Innsmouth" the central character is more and more fascinated by the horrors he has witnessed. He had long struggled—and how energetically!— to escape from the vaguely anthropomorphic beings that inspired in him so natural a revulsion. But scarcely does he find himself in safety than he passionately scrutinizes familial archives, examines old manuscripts, rereads hoary letters. . . . There was an uncle Douglas who committed suicide . . . a cousin Lawrence who was locked up in an asylum. . . . And finally he understands what has always been hidden from him: by his maternal great-grandmother he is related to the monsters! The blood of the Deep Ones runs in his veins! Each day he more distinctly develops the "Innsmouth look"!

But far from wanting to end his existence, he little by little becomes accustomed to the modifications in his features, the transformation of his bearing. No, he will not kill himself; he will free his cousin and the two will rejoin their venerable grandmother at the bottom of that marine gulf off Innsmouth. They will swim for ever amid the phosphorescent marvels of the great depths, between the Cyclopean columns of glorious Y'ha-nthlei: *Iä!-R'lyeh! Cthulhu fhtagn! Iä! Iä!* At the end of this slow evolution, this prodigious *metanoia*, the abominable, the repugnant, the unclean have become not only natural but desirable. The fantastic here is perhaps not so much the physical transformation of the narrator as this extraordinary change of heart. How many characters, suddenly touched by a type of malefic grace, stricken by a spell from the past, are thus metamorphosed! Pickman, that mad painter whose hideous art scandalizes virtuous Boston, day by day takes on a more repulsive, a more *animal* cast; this, at any rate, is what alarms his friend Reid, a specialist in "comparative pathology."[5] Does not Pickman himself have among his ancestors some dubious characters? A witch, in particular, hanged in Salem in 1692. . . . His final disappearance surprises no one, and much relieves the members of his social circle. But what has he become? Randolph Carter meets him later, on the other side of the Gate of Deeper Slumber:

> There, on a tombstone of 1768 stolen from the Granary Burying Ground in Boston, sat the ghoul which was once the artist Richard Upton Pickman. It was naked and rubbery, and had acquired so much of the ghoulish physiognomy that its human origin was already obscure. But it still remembered a little English, and was able to converse with Carter in grunts and monosyllables, helped out now and then by the glibbering of ghouls.[6]

Lovecraft's characters are, indeed, *mutants*, but of a very different type from those with which science fiction presents us. Far from being determined by the *evolution* of the race, they are dominated by their familial *antecedents*. It is at the end of a *regressive* process that Pickman becomes a ghoul, or another such hero, a Deep One, a process that must be placed in the perspective of a manifestly decadent esthetic, inspired—or aggravated—by the author's personal phantasms.

If in most cases the characters resign themselves to the ineluctable, submit passively to their fate, or go eagerly to their downfall, it sometimes happens that their belonging to a dubious lineage leads to tragedy. Arthur Jermyn cannot reconcile himself to his destiny after he makes some discoveries. Doubtless it is easy to accept in the abstract the truth taught by naturalists—that man is descended from monkeys. It is, however, more difficult to learn without losing one's head that one's grandmother was a chimp— even though white and advanced. . . . "Life is a hideous thing," says the narrator at the beginning of the tale, "and from the background behind what we know of it peer demoniacal hints of truth which make it sometimes a thousandfold more hideous."[7] The capture of the consciousness is made by stages: troubling, alarming, terrifying signs accumulate. And when doubt no longer remains, when a parcel received from Africa confirms the most frightful suspicions, there is nothing more to do than to pour gasoline on oneself and burn oneself alive.

And yet, to the very end and despite the horror of the situation, Arthur Jermyn maintains an entirely British dignity; his last act harms only himself. It is entirely otherwise with the sinister hero of "The Rats in the Walls." This tale illustrates in a still more typically *American* way than the others this return to genealogical origins. The de la Poers, living in the United States since the seventeenth century, have totally broken off with their past. The drama begins at the moment the last descendant of this illustrious family of rich Massachusetts industrialists buys back the ancestral Exham Priory after World War I and settles into it. Intrigued, then alarmed, by nocturnal noises that seem to come from the cellar, he explores the subterranean tunnels of this ancient dwelling, accompanied by trustworthy and competent associates. We have seen how the depths of the house are also the depths of the past. Does the term "house" not, moreover, at the same time designate architecture and the family line? This has been well exhibited by Poe in "The Fall of the House of Usher."

We have previously spoken of this expedition and have left de la Poer in a cave dug under the foundations of his restored castle, at the moment he realizes that the mass of human debris that surrounds him is the remains of impious feasts in which his own ancestors had taken part. It is then that the inconceivable takes place. This respectable industrialist, this quinquagenerian incarnating all the virtues of his class, suddenly loses all restraints and gives way irresistibly to horrid instincts surging from the abysmal depths of racial memory: *"Magna Mater! Magna Mater!"* howls this man who a little earlier had spoken so rationally. *"Atys . . . Dia ad aghaid's ad aodaun . . . agus bas leat-sa! . . . Ungl . . . ungl . . . rrlh . . . chch. . . ."*[8] Later we find him bent over the *half-eaten* cadaver of one of his learned friends.

We can, to be sure, cite other tales where execrable voices emerge from a faraway past to dictate demented actions to the characters; but it would not add greatly to our analysis.

What is important to emphasize is this horror of familial antecedents in Lovecraft, of the secret taint that, in precise cases, reactivates sleeping tendencies, suddenly brings out certain traits, and transforms—in the most material sense of the term—the characters. These obsessive images, which seem to be imposed so strongly on the author, are too numerous and too carefully articulated to be explained away as simple literary effect. Can we from now on completely avoid imputing them to the more or less clear consciousness that Lovecraft had of his own heredity? Everything centers, in sum, on the crucial problem of corrupted blood. And this child of a paretic perhaps had some legitimate reasons for giving way to an anguished reverie on the ever possible perturbation of hereditary patrimony and the regrettable transmission of acquired characteristics.

If the fantastic is game, artifice, gratuitous construction, its quality depends on how it is anchored in reality. The perfect command, which never leaves Lovecraft when he spins the web of his tales, the minute detail and rigor with which he builds his intrigues, and the apparent objectivity in which he envelops his remarks are clearly proofs of his art, but also a sure indication of an attempt to dramatize, and consequently to overcome, intimate conflicts. It might even be said that his whole oeuvre could be read as the pathetic journal of a cure, or of an attempt at a cure; we will have occasion to return to this.

7
CTHULHU

So from the wells of night to the gulfs of space, and from the gulfs of space to the wells of night, ever the praises of Great Cthulhu, of Tsathoggua, and of Him Who is not to be Named.

— "The Whisperer in Darkness"[1]

At the risk of shocking or deceiving we would like here to repeat, before going any further in our analysis, how Lovecraft's tales seem to us distinct from science fiction. The cosmic dimension of the settings, the "entities" from Outside, and the scientific experiments were for Lovecraft a means, not an end: the oftentimes feeble pretext for a reverie where space and time are arranged very differently.

Science fiction is basically a forward-looking genre, preoccupied with the future, where anguish is projected in forms conceived from the data of the then current science. In a way it is a dream that

79

outruns science and, from embryonic elements, invents what scholars and technologists establish or rigorously create later. In a science fiction tale the imaginary always runs the risk of descending to the real.[2]

Lovecraft's art, however, is essentially regressive, oriented toward a fabulous past and rooted in myth. In this it is an authentically fantastic art, forever belonging to the realm of chimeras and the unverifiable. We might even be tempted to say that the fantastic is, on the axis of the imagination, rigorously opposed to science fiction.[3]

In science fiction tales the cosmos is a virgin space, a space to be conquered, a place of sublimation; time is time to come. In Lovecraft, space is perceived as a void, a depth; time, as the mythical time of beginnings. And in the depths of time, at the other end of the cosmos, horror lurks. It is not man who will recklessly explore new worlds with prodigious machines; it is the Unknown, which, under diverse yet always unholy forms, breaks out on our planet. The initiative is not on the side of the human race, which instead serves as the field of observation and . . . experimentation for fabulously different beings who are phenomenally more advanced scientifically and technologically than man.

In Lovecraft, knowledge and technical efficiency are not found at the end of human evolution, but at the beginning. For him, the notion of progress, in the modern sense of the term, is devoid of meaning. On the contrary, the history of the civilizations that from time immemorial have followed one another on our planet has been one of a slow and irreversible decadence. Contemporary man is not defined by his future conquests of space or by his ever growing mastery of natural phenomena, but as one who has lost what the Great Old Ones knew before him. Coming from deep regions of the ether, these primordial beings established themselves on the earth millions of years before man ever appeared. If we believe the narrator of *At the Mountains of Madness,* they were infinitely more advanced than we in technology, art, and basic research. They were able to conceive and create docile slaves, who obeyed their hypnotic suggestions and built marvelous cities for them. They were strong, wise, and happy. And only the revolt of the shoggoths, unforeseeable and devastating, could end this model civilization.

For the dreamer from Providence, *the beginning, the elsewhere,* was perfection. Since *that* time, on *this* world, wretched humanity, having forgotten everything, is overwhelmed, devoured, dominated by these unknown forces it can no longer understand. It is because Lovecraft built his whole work on this mythical, irrational base that he is not, in our eyes, an author of science fiction. The Cthulhu Mythos, which each of his tales resumes and treats with greater or less amplitude, is incompatible with the hyperrationality that characterizes the genre illustrated today by Poul Anderson, Ray Bradbury, and many other lesser writers. To sum up in a few words what clearly merits a more thorough study, let us say that myth and science, in fiction as in everything else, are mutually exclusive.

But perhaps it is time to examine this myth, which firmly structures the Lovecraft oeuvre and gives it its significance. "All my stories," wrote the author, "are based on the fundamental premise that common laws and interests and emotions have no validity or significance in the vast cosmos-at-large. . . . To achieve the essence of real externality, whether of time or space or dimension, one must forget that such things as good and evil, love and hate, and all such local attributes of a negligible and temporary race called mankind, have any existence at all."[4]

By making some comparisons and tests, it is possible to reconstruct a vast fresco, a cosmic-dimensioned "saga" in which each tale would represent an episode. The obvious drawback in this procedure is in rationalizing what in essence ought not to be rationalized. Moreover, the Cthulhu Mythos is not the exclusive work of Lovecraft; others have contributed to it—his friends and disciples Clark Ashton Smith, Frank Belknap Long, Robert E. Howard, August Derleth, Robert Bloch the scenarist, and many others, each creating and animating new characters. But it may be useful to shed some light, for practical ends, on this unheard-of jumble of baffling images and forms. At the risk of some omissions and a few contradictions, let us see how this universal myth can, if reconstructed, be read.

At the summit of this diabolical hierarchy we must name Azathoth, the "blind and idiot" god. Installed at the heart of Ultimate Chaos, it is he who presides over human destiny; in this way is the radical absurdity of the world explained. Like the gods of Dunsany to whom they owe so much, Lovecraft's gods are transparent allegories, and Azathoth illustrates adequately the author's theses on mechanistic materialism. He is, for the dreamer Randolph Carter who is searching for marvelous Kadath, that shocking final peril which gibbers unmentionably outside the ordered universe, where no dreams reach; that last amorphous blight of nethermost confusion which blasphemes and bubbles at the centre of all infinity—the boundless daemon-sultan Azathoth, whose name no lips dare speak aloud, and who gnaws hungrily in inconceivable, unlighted chambers beyond time amidst the muffled, maddening beat of vile drums and the thin, monotonous whine of accursed flutes; to which detestable pounding and piping dance slowly, awkwardly, and absurdly the gigantic ultimate gods, the blind, voiceless, tenebrous, and mindless Other Gods whose soul and messenger is the crawling chaos Nyarlathotep.[5]

Nyarlathotep is the faithful servant of Azathoth. He is most often designated vaguely, such as the "Crawling Chaos." But he has many other names: he is sometimes the "Dark God," sometimes "The Dweller in Darkness," sometimes "The Faceless God," or again "The Howler in the Night." His most notable appearance is made in "The Haunter of the Dark," in the form of a jet-black "flying thing" who, emitting an intense stench, is endowed with an enormous three-lobed eye, which throws off a deadly light. He is invoked and worshipped in this form, by means of the Shining Trapezohedron, in the steeple of an old church in Providence, where his appearance in a night storm strews panic. But he can take on other aspects: In *The Dream-Quest of Unknown Kadath* he appears to Randolph Carter in the form of a young man of great beauty, clothed in the austere dignity of an Egyptian god and in a scarlet robe. . . .[6]

As redoubtable, as strong as Azathoth, is Yog-Sothoth, the All-in-One, the One-in-All, also coming from the stars. The myth tells us that he resembles a conglomeration of sparkling globules agglutinated one to the other. It is of him that the archaic *Book of Eibon*[7] speaks, it is to him that the hideous *Necronomicon* sings its praises. It is he who is invoked in the symbolic formulas of Charles Dexter Ward, it is he who has engendered the double horror at Dunwich. "Nor is it to be thought," we read in the terrible opus of the mad Arab Abdul Alhazred,

that man is either the oldest or the last of earth's masters. . . . The Old Ones were, the Old Ones are, and the Old Ones shall be. Not in the spaces we know, but *between* them, They walk serene and primal, undimensioned and to us unseen. *Yog-Sothoth* knows the gate. *Yog-Sothoth* is the gate. *Yog-Sothoth* is the key and the guardian of the gate. Past, present, future, all are one in *Yog-Sothoth*. He knows where the Old Ones broke through of old, and where They shall break through again. . . . *Yog-Sothoth* is the key of the gate, whereby the spheres meet. Man rules where They ruled once; They shall soon rule where Man rules now.[8]

It is Yog-Sothoth whom the crustacean-bodied creatures of "The Whisperer in Darkness" worship, it is he whom Joseph Curwen frequently invokes in the course of his abominable experiments. He has existed for all time, he is everywhere at once, he is unclean and cruel. He is the Guardian of the Ultimate Gate.

With Yog-Sothoth, Cthulhu is perhaps the deity most often evoked by Lovecraft's characters. While Yog-Sothoth wanders the Outer Spaces, Cthulhu has by accident been imprisoned in a monument of ancient R'lyeh, the city engulfed in the Pacific. Like Yog-Sothoth he came from the stars and now "reposes" in the sea. His aspect is vaguely anthropomorphic; but he has an octopus-head and, instead of a face, a mass of swarming tentacles. His body, covered with scales, has a rubbery consistency. His paws are armed with prodigious claws, and he has long, narrow wings on his back. His worshippers, who by chance happen to be *degenerate half-breeds*,[9] observe a changeless rite and from generation to generation ever chant the same verse: "Ph'nglui mglw'nafh Cthulhu R'lyeh wgah'nagl fhtagn." This, as the readers of "The Call of Cthulhu" well know, means: "In his house at R'lyeh dead Cthulhu waits dreaming."[10] But although these incantations and the barbarous rites accompanying them remained inefficacious millennium after millennium, the simple curiosity of sailors threatened to unleash this horror on the world. When Johansen and his companions disembarked on the unknown island that had surged from the waves after an upheaval of deep land masses, they saw that from the bottom of a black pit, where the very darkness seemed to have become viscous, some indescribable "Thing"[11] was coming alive that endangered their reason and their lives. It was Cthulhu, the Great Old One, the fallen deity, who with Dagon rules over all that swarms at the bottom of the sea.

Dagon does not in this Pantheon of Horror occupy the same place as the Great Old Ones. He is certainly the servant of Cthulhu, as Nyarlathotep is of Azathoth. He is no less the master of the Deep Ones, the half-fishy, half-batrachian beings who live in the marvelous cities of the great deeps, but who when they wish can easily venture upon the land and mate with humans. We know already that at Innsmouth there is a sect of the "Esoteric Order of Dagon" whose priests wear tiaras and who under the folds of their ample vestments hide singular deformities. . . . Lovecraft nowhere gives a precise description of Dagon, and perhaps this is for the best. At most, in the tale with the name of this redoubtable entity for its title, we are shown from afar a gigantic silhouette with enormous scaly arms, which gropes after a lunatic monolith erected in a nightmare landscape.[12] . . . It is a monolith whose base is ornamented with frescoes representing unclean beings, roughly human but with webbed hands and feet, flabby lips, and protruding, glassy eyes. When Dagon has been met but once in one's existence, even drugs ease not the burden of life: The narrator of "Dagon," at the end of his tether, commits suicide, to escape—so he believes—that whose massive and viscous presence he senses behind the door of his room.

The other gods who people and animate Lovecraft's mythical universe, though they are physically as repulsive, seem less dangerous to men. Among them let us mention 'Umr at-Tawil, dean of the Great Old Ones and direct servant of Yog-Sothoth; Tsathoggua, the Toad-God, potbellied, hairy, and swarthy, settled on the earth since its creation and originating from the planet Cykranosh;[13] the gigantic Ghatanothoa, imprisoned since his rebellion in the crypts of the fortress constructed by the "crustaceans" of Yuggoth at the summit of Mount Yaddith-Gho;[14] and Shub-Niggurath, wife of Yog-Sothoth, the Black Goat of the Woods, of whom it is said in the *Necronomicon* that she will proliferate hideously throughout the world.

Such are the actors of a drama that, having the Cosmos for its stage, unfolds in the tales of H. P. Lovecraft. It is a drama where man seems to have no other role than to act as victim—terrorized, mutilated, tossed from one corner of the universe to the other. Indeed, the old legends themselves have set down in fable man's destiny; and Lovecraft, who as a child played at building altars in honor of pagan deities, knew it well. Dunsany, whom Lovecraft idolized, had on his part often conceived, in *The Gods of Pegāna* and other collections of fantastic tales, divinities with exotic names, such as Māna-Yood-Sushāi, the God who created the gods; Slid whose soul is in the sea; Mung the God of Death; and Loharneth-Lahai, God of Fantasy, who spends eternity in dream. Let us, however, agree that neither the familiar gods of classical mythology nor the slightly decadent gods of the Irish poet have the odious and fascinating presence of those invented by Lovecraft. The first enhance the tragic sense of life that underlies ancient philosophy; the second belong to a fantasy world where the imagination of poets of the "Yellow Nineties" readily took refuge. Lovecraft's gods, however, are fantastic because they are manifested in daily reality, outside the author's every belief, every adherence to a dogma or church. Surging from dream-depths, they settle into the Waking World, mingle and mate with humans, and inflict a thousand experiments upon them. Yet somehow the Great Old Ones *need* men; for it is, as we will see, by man's adoration that they can hope to liberate themselves and return to the earth in all their glory.

8
UNHOLY CULTS

Y'AI 'NG'NGAH
YOG-SOTHOTH
H'EE—L'BEG
F'AI THRODOG
UAAAH![1]

In a book that the celebrated magician Harry Houdini suggested that he write, Lovecraft about 1925 proposed to reveal—in a land where witches had been hanged—the errors of superstition, magic, and the irrational beliefs to which a feeble humanity is ever addicted.

The book was not written, but there survives a detailed enough outline, prepared by Lovecraft with his usual minuteness. This project, entitled *The Cancer of Superstition*, included a study of the genesis of the phenomenon of superstitious belief, a denunciation of the animism of primitive societies, and an erudite note—interesting for our purposes—on how we invent myths and cosmogonies through the centuries.[2]

We thus cannot imagine that the Cthulhu Mythos, elaborated as it was by one who had read Fiske and Frazer, could have been the result of a naive, spontaneous act, implying the least faith in the characters described or the phenomena reported. Yog-Sothoth has manifestly been created by a complete skeptic. We cannot overemphasize the author's attitude of perfect, total, and definitive incredulity concerning the numinous, illustrated here by his fervent desire to wrestle with the seemingly many and varied survivals of superstition in the century of Einstein. To make Lovecraft—and it seems that such a temptation is great among some of his readers—a follower of some secret society or a high priest of some unheard-of and obscure religious sect would not only be to ignore the man as he was, but greatly to err on the significance and import of his oeuvre, an oeuvre that is fantastic precisely inasmuch as he himself has ceased to believe in the supernatural. As has excellently been shown by Louis Vax,[3] fantastic literature is necessarily the daughter of unbelief.[4]

This is the reason that the scenes of sorcery, the sabbaths, the Walpurgis-nights, which give Lovecraft's tales their special coloration, are captivating and frightening to the twentieth-century reader: the tales are rooted not in belief but in the imagination, and obey laws of artistic creation that are, we repeat, to an extent a gratuitous play and diversion. This does not mean, certainly, that these obsessive images cannot have a profound significance; we shall consider this later on.

For truly there is in Lovecraft an obsession with infamy and sacrilege which rests on an inverted aesthetic, what one can almost call a systematization of transgression. The irruption of the irrational, which is a violation of intelligence, ought also to be the contravention of aesthetic norms; the unintelligible is necessarily hideous. We also find in some tales a theogony, a liturgy, a ritual, which expresses and actualizes the mythical abstractions previously noted. Lovecraft the agnostic felt the need to build a dogma supported, as all rational systems are, by knowledge recorded in books, treatises, and reference works.

In the first rank of these manuals, which it cannot be without interest to present rapidly to the reader, we should cite a book that has often before been noted, the *Necronomicon*. It acts as a veritable

Bible, written by the mad Arab Abdul Alhazred, who lived in Yemen about A.D. 700. If Lovecraft, who later wrote a "History of the *Necronomicon*,"[5] is to be believed, Alhazred had brought back from the ruins of Babylon and the depths of Memphis, and also from the great Arabia Deserta where he had sojourned for six years, hideous secrets concerning the Great Old Ones, Yog-Sothoth and Cthulhu. "Tradition" states that he had recorded these secrets in a manuscript *bound in human skin* before abruptly disappearing—some say before being devoured by an invisible monster.

The book, translated into Greek in the tenth century by Theodorus Philetas of Constantinople, inspired secret and catastrophic experiences over the generations. Put on the Index, burned by order of the Patriarch Michael in 1050, it is found again two centuries later in a Latin translation. Printed in the fifteenth century in Germany and in the seventeenth in Spain, the editions were each time destroyed almost entirely by religious authorities. Only very few copies escaped the zeal of the Inquisitors and are today accessible in great national libraries. The book was cited in so many tales and each time with such seriousness that there were many readers, if we believe August Derleth,[6] who wrote to the British Museum asking for the tome.

Next to the *Necronomicon*, in a respected position we find the Pnakotic Manuscripts. Only some scant initiates among men have been able, without losing their reason, to translate and understand these texts, which deal with the Great Old Ones and the other gods of primeval times.

Of the *Seven Cryptical Books of Hsan* we know not a great deal, except that there is a single copy of it in the locked and inaccessible vault of the Library of Miskatonic University in Arkham and that to read it is particularly dangerous.

As for the *Book of Eibon*, it is particularly devoted to the cult of Tsathoggua, and contains singularly malefic incantations.[7]

The Book of Thoth, finally, is never cited directly.[8] Is it perhaps too hideous for that? But Alhazred makes allusions to it in the *Necronomicon*, and such homage is not negligible. . . .

Next to manuscripts—all prodigiously ancient except the *Necronomicon*—Lovecraft often makes reference here and there to "modern" works on magic, such as the *Cultes des Goules* of the Comte d'Erlette,[9] the *Unaussprechlichen Kulten* of von Junzt,[10] the

Image du Monde of Gautier de Metz,[11] and the "celebrated" *Liber Damnatus,* which Joseph Curwen is inspired by so often and so . . . efficaciously in *The Case of Charles Dexter Ward.*[12]

This esoteric literature constitutes a sort of modern "gloss" on the Old Texts, a commentary that corresponds, in the supposed authors, to an obvious desire to catechize. Above all, these books amplify the mystery that carefully surrounds the primitive manuscripts and confirm their authenticity in the reader's eye. If necessary, Lovecraft drops among these purely fictitious titles the names of some real works—chosen, it is true, with particular care—such as the *Daemonolatreia* of Remigius, which appeared at Lyons in 1595, the well-known *Saducismus Triumphatus* of Joseph Glanvil, and the horrible but perfectly authentic *De Masticatione Mortuorum* of Philippus Rohr, published in Leipzig in 1679. Thus, a credibility colors these most improbable pages.

The Great Old Ones have thus permitted man, through these books, to attain their secrets. But if many are called, few are chosen. The church founded by them on earth allows, as do all churches, a mob of anonymous and faithful worshippers to be satisfied by superficial and blind ritual. Such are all those degenerates, all those half-breeds and half-wits who send up to Them barbarous incantations and the acrid smoke of dubious sacrifices. Strange in truth is the church where Persians and Mongols, Indians and Negroes, savages from faraway islands and newly (often clandestinely) arrived immigrants mix in the slums of the great cities; some are grotesquely rigged up in ill-fitting, loud-colored clothes or dressed in obsolete rags signifying their connections with utterly bygone times, others dancing completely naked and howling in the depths of tropical forests. All are the heirs of prodigiously old traditions and are manifestly ill-adapted to modern civilization. They form, at the heart of American society, irreducible, unassimilable nuclei, which menace it from within. These harmful communities, such as the Esoteric Order of Dagon, the hoary sect of the Yezidis, or the dead and silent crowd of "The Festival," have their own priests, their own altars, their own prophets. Their members worship in deconsecrated churches or in secret crypts, led in their devotions by clerics adorned with the sacerdotal ornaments of their rank. Satanism, though this term is too benign, even ludicrous, to serve for such rites, also has its structure and its hierarchy.

It also has its "initiates," its "elect": these are the alchemists, very special "sorcerers" who reach, after an entire life of close commerce with the *Necronomicon*, a degree of initiation that allows for stupefying actualizations. Joseph Curwen, Ephraim Waite, and Robert Suydam are the ageless men who perpetuate themselves from century to century, prevented only by the ingenuity of a few normal beings from realizing their projects. Yet it seldom happens, ultimately, that their fellow citizens succeed in totally eliminating them; a high-priest of Yog-Sothoth cannot entirely die. When the eminent citizens of Providence make Joseph Curwen "disappear," they are far from suspecting that the long-lived spirit of their "victim" will settle two centuries later into a young and vigorous body. And did the unfortunate Edward Derby know when he married Asenath Waite that he had bound his destiny with that of old Ephraim, the sinister old man who, lacking a male descendant, provisionally settled into the body of his daughter while coveting the more comfortable and convenient form of the young man. . . ? Under the expert pen of the author, having himself just had the depersonalizing experience of an unhappy marriage, this old motif of vampiric possession resumes surprisingly vivid colors. Here again the sorcerer's demonic will is exercized beyond the tomb, and the young aesthete of Arkham ends his existence in the nauseating form that we all know. While the initiate assimilates this entirely new life and thus recovers his strength, a body in an advanced state of putrefaction—one might say half-liquid—collapses "on the doorstep" in a viscous and brownish pool. The spectacular rejuvenation of Robert Suydam, in "The Horror at Red Hook," is explained in the same way, at the very moment the many abductions of children throw New York into consternation. His marriage is just as equivocal; and tongues fly at a good clip when it is learned that the young wife has died on her wedding day. What, indeed, could have happened? And why is the poor girl's body *completely bloodless*? The author decidedly has a bad opinion of conjugal habits, implying that one of the spouses will necessarily end entirely drained of his or her own substance.

According to Lovecraft, the alchemist is a demoniac character, cold as the tomb, timeless, cruel, and full of artifice. After execrable experiments, the results of which he shares with his several confreres who reside at various points on the globe, he metamorphoses himself or disappears with disconcerting ease. The *Nec-*

ronomicon is his bedside book, Yog-Sothoth his supreme interlocutor, the renewal of his lease among the living his sole preoccupation. Divided between his laboratory and his singular devotions, he incarnates at once the ultimate deviation of the intellect and the absolute perversion of the heart. Serving as dubious mediator between infamous deities and a corrupted humanity, he from century to century perpetuates a total evil.

What a difference from the great demoniacs of the past who, having once signed the pact, survive disgustingly and despairingly! Neither Godwin's St. Leon nor Shelley's Zastrozzi or the Rosicrucian St. Irvyne, nor yet the sad Melmoth of the Reverend Maturin has the unclean presence of a Joseph Curwen or an Ephraim Waite. Molded from a Christian culture, their desire for infinite knowledge changes immediately into remorse as soon as it has been fulfilled. Having rapidly exhausted the superficial pleasures that power and riches give them, they lead a miserable existence and soon aspire to the death that they have paid so dearly to postpone. What a difference, too, from the noble, terrible, and generous Zanoni of Bulwer-Lytton, who by love renounces his terrible power! As for the modern sorcerers conceived by Jean Ray or Seignolles, what could they possibly have in common with the hirelings of Cthulhu, whose impiety extends, let us repeat, infinitely beyond ordinary satanism and popular tradition?

This appears yet more clearly in the celebrations of those demented cults over which the sorcerers preside. Their "interlocutor," at the heart of these ceremonies utterly unparalleled in all fantastic literature, is not the devil of legend, but one of those primordial and mythical beings of whom we have elsewhere spoken. Satan has not survived this fundamental mutation of the imagination brought about, even in the land of Puritanism, by the secularization of the conscience: He is as dead as God.

The places where the cult meets inspire, perhaps, more revulsion than fear. They are, we have seen, places of the deep—crypts, caves, subterranean grottoes—which plunge into the thick darkness that is the very substance of dream. Through the smoke of incense, or of things giving off less reputable fumes, move forms about whose humanity or completeness we are never sure, in the glimmer of torches brandished by imprecise silhouettes. Harshly sonorous chants and incantations alternate with collective gesticulations, dances with rhythms more and more delirious, all of which is completed in a frenetic apotheosis of noise, movement, and horror.

Then the abomination emerges. In "The Horror at Red Hook" its name is Lilith, a gelatinous and phosphorescent monstrosity before whom all bow, completely naked. In "The Festival" it is a column of primordial fire, which, through mephitic vapours and amid amorphous presences crouching in the half-light, is adored by a hypnotized crowd and by flying, hybrid, indescribable monsters. Or again there are the hordes of degenerates who, in "The Call of Cthulhu," gesticulate and howl like the possessed around the effigy of the Great Old One, raised on a gigantic granite monolith. Elsewhere we find nocturnal sabbaths in a megalithic site or on the top of a hill, and in "The Dreams in the Witch House" we are present at the sacrifice of a child and at barbarous rites during which blood served in a golden cup circulates in a more conventional manner among the guests.

Most often the sacrifices are not described but suggested by the disappearance of children or the discovery of curious bones. There is little doubt, however, that these unheard-of ceremonies all conclude with propitiary offerings. In "The Horror at Red Hook" it is the sinister Robert Suydam who, having played with fire for too long, is offered in oblation. It is of little importance that he is already dead—this is at least what he seems to be—when an infernal saraband of lemurs, fauns, and incubi forms around his body and raises execrable chants to the deity. It is also of little importance that the "victim" of the sacrifice, complete corpse that he seems to be, is not consenting and tries to flee as quickly as his members, already stricken with corruption, allow; he will cave in soon, for the delight of Lilith, into a mass of putrid flesh.

The incantations and the magical formulas play no negligible role, we suspect, at the heart of these singular gatherings. They are chanted in languages at once strange and ancient, as one might expect in these "babels of sound and filth,"[13] which is what the slums of the great cities have become, where so many different races mix. The fantastic is not only the rout of intelligence; it is also a linguistic bewilderment. When Malone is present at the cult of Lilith in the secret crypts of Red Hook, he hears the chanting of verses that he knows to be the most infamous prayer ever invented by Greek decadence in contact with Judaism: "HEL. HELOYM. SOTHER. EMMANVEL. SABAOTH. AGLA. TETRAGRAM-

MATON. AGYROS. OTHEOS. ISCHYROS. ATHANATOS. IEHOVA. VA. ADONAI. SADAY. HOMOVSION. MESSIAS. ESCHEREHEYE."[14]

If the reader here or there identifies some term, he happily does not understand the message. It is the same in *The Case of Charles Dexter Ward,* when the young man's parents hear these phrases intoned strongly behind the door of his room:

> *Per Adonai Eloim, Adonai Jehova*
> *Adonai Sabaoth, Metraton On Agla Methon,*
> *Verbum pythonicum, mysterium salamandrae,*
> *conventus sylvorum, antra gnomorum,*
> *daemonia Coeli God, Almonsin, Gibor, Jehosua,*
> *Evam, Zariatnatmik, veni, veni, veni.*[15]

In contrast with his predecessors in the fantastic tradition, Lovecraft was not content to mention these ritualistic recitations; he took pleasure in *composing* them. His ear was as finely developed as his sense of smell, and the anomalies of language, just as the corruption of bodies, seemed to him potentially disquieting. Very sensitive to the diabolic quality of certain sounds, he never missed making allusion to them when the occasion presented itself:

> Only poetry or madness could do justice to the noise heard by Legrasse's men as they ploughed through the black morass toward the red glare and the muffled tom-toms. There are vocal qualities peculiar to men, and vocal qualities peculiar to beasts; and it is terrible to hear the one when the source should yield the other. Animal fury and orgiastic licence here whipped themselves to daemoniac heights by howls and squawking ecstasies that tore and reverberated through those nighted woods like pestilential tempests from the gulfs of hell.[16]

We see again that the author, wanting the better to translate the horror of these primitive exclamations, projects upon them an image of depth. Language, like the whole visible universe, has its infrastructure.

Sometimes the words, just as the flesh of many of his victims, decompose, liquefy, and flow in nauseating chants from impure lips: "Ph'nglui mglw'nafh Cthulhu R'lyeh wgah'nagl fhtagn," sing the worshippers of Cthulhu, while the invisible Dunwich horror cries out before dying: "Ygnaiih . . . ygnaiih . . . thflthkh'ngha . . . Yog-Sothoth . . . Y'bthnk . . . h'ehye—n'grkdl'lh."[17]

As for the mysterious formulas Charles Ward uses in his dangerous experiments, they analogously reveal that the rapports with the Beyond take place through the disintegration, the disarticulation of familiar language. To evoke the "Outsiders," one must say:

> Y'AI 'NG'NGAH
> *YOG-SOTHOTH*
> H'EE—L'BEG
> F'AI—THRODOG
> *UAAAH*

And to send them back into nothingness, we need only restate the formula in reverse:

> OGTHROD AI'F
> GEB'L—EE'H
> *YOG-SOTHOTH*
> 'NGAH'NG AI'Y
> *ZHRO*[18]

Truly a handy formula! For when Dr. Willett completes its recitation, Joseph Curwen is scattered over the ground, now merely a fine layer of bluish-gray dust.

In Lovecraft, fantastic creation rests on the destruction of all structures, those of language as well as those of space and time.

But the author was not content to create these unholy celebrations and blasphemous incantations. In taking care to elaborate this reverse theogony of which we have already spoken, he went still further: not only is this religion of the Great Old Ones a *revealed* religion, based on prophetic writings that constitute a sort of inverse biblical culture, but more it is a religion that essentially rests on the central phenomenon of incarnation.

But what incarnation! We must here make note of the hybrid "entities" of Innsmouth, fruits of the monstrous coupling of Deep Ones with humans, and particularly the unclean progeny of Yog-Sothoth in "The Dunwich Horror." This tale is the unbearable story of a reverse gospel, an inverse history of salvation. A primordial deity has been incarnated in Wilbur; a Great Old One has been made a man. Such is the result of old Whateley's practices, which seek to reestablish on earth the reign of the Old Ones, as predicted in the *Necronomicon*. To those who question him about his daughter's offspring, he usually replies with a prophecy. "Some day," he says, "yew folks'll hear a child o' Lavinny's a-callin' its father's name on the top o' Sentinel Hill!"[19] But instead of being an apocalypse, the final scene can be read as the replica, in the horrific mode, of the story of the Passion. At the moment Armitage pronounces the fateful verses, which will send Wilbur's twin brother back into nothingness, *the darkness grows, lightning tears the sky*, and before dying the invisible Son of Yog-Sothoth cries: "*Ey-ya-ya-ya-e'yayayayaaaa . . . ngh'aaaa . . . ngh'aaaa. . .* h'yuh . . . h'yuh . . . HELP! HELP! . . . *ff-ff-ff*-FATHER! FATHER! YOG-SOTHOTH!"[20] thus echoing the "Eloi, Eloi, Lamma Sabachtani" of the Gospels.

If the Miskatonic University librarian had been any less vigilant or less competent, Lavinia Whateley, humble human Virgin, would have been the instrument for the final return to glory on our planet of Yog-Sothoth, the Great Old One, the deity who came from the stars in the immemorial times of Cthulhu and Tsathoggua.

The fantastic for Lovecraft is not only this oneiric upsetting of the world, which we have previously mentioned; it is also, on a moral plane, the inversion of values, the destruction of all that has an integrating and stabilizing function in society. In the universal collapse, nothing can be saved that would allow man to orient himself, not even the sacred, which must become the sacrilegious.

9

IN THE CHASMS OF DREAM

. . . into the smoke-wreathed world of dream.
—"The Haunter of the Dark"[1]

In the preceding pages we have frequently emphasized the dreamlike quality of the images that makes Lovecraft's writing what it is. Images of the spiral staircase, the labyrinth, the subterranean cave, and stagnant water are the "psychic hieroglyphs" whose significance—if, indeed, it is essential or possible to invest them with a clear meaning—must be sought at the innermost levels of abysmal life. It seems just as evident that the thick, consistent darkness in which the characters carry out their destinies is the same dark depth into which the dreamer plunges.

Lovecraft tells us in his letters—and nothing indicates that their veracity is to be doubted—how some tales were written immediately upon waking, from the still vivid memories of a dream. Thus, "The Statement of Randolph Carter" is an almost literal transcription of a dream in which the author saw himself, along with his friend and correspondent, Samuel Loveman, exploring one of the old New England cemeteries of which he was so fond. The adventures which lay in wait for the two men—Loveman's descent into a vault, the contact he established by telephone with Lovecraft who stayed on the surface, the frightful denouement—all this was already in the dream.[2] "Nyarlathotep" is a scarcely more dramatized nightmare whose beginning, the author tells us, was written even before he was fully awake.[3] "Celephaïs" is a fabric of dreams laid end to end,[4] and the tales of the Randolph Carter cycle, of which we shall soon speak, are all placed entirely under the sign of "Hypnos," the god who gives his name to one of the author's most immaterial and most terrible tales.

"I never *try* to write a story," he tells us, "but wait till it *has to be* written."[5] And these compelling impulses were communicated to him by his dreams. When he tried to write by forcing himself, the result was flat and cold. He knew not how to compose a worthwhile tale except under the incitement of dream. He even carried this scruple to the point of wondering whether those works he wrote in this other state ought truly to be considered his own.[6]

Certainly Lovecraft would have us believe that his whole life, and certainly his youth and adolescence, was spent in an intense dream-activity. The dreams he describes in his letters—those he has not dramatized in his stories—strike us by their somber and disquieting character. He dreamed of solitary houses, Gothic castles, endless stairways, black and inimical beasts with rubbery and smooth bodies,[7] streets on the summit of a slope suddenly open on to a starry abysm.[8] . . . He dreamed of statuettes that he had shaped and for which a curator of a museum offered a fabulous price.[9] . . . He dreamed that he was falling in an endless and dark space, peopled with surly voices and menacing presences. . . . He dreamed that he was a centurion in the era when the Roman legions were established in Spain.[10] He dreamed of marvelous cities whose domes and minarets glittered in the dying rays of a setting sun. He dreamed of mountainous sites, inaccessible heights, muddy swamps, and faceless men whose heads were made of a whitish cone surmounted by a blood-red tentacle.[11] . . . But it would be pointless to enumerate all the dreams that, not without some childish complacence, he describes in those voluminous missives in which a psychoanalyst would delight.

98

If dreams occupied an important place in Lovecraft's life, they play a hardly less negligible role in the lives of his characters. We can note that the author's dream that inspired a tale is often introduced in the tale initially as a dream. The process is as old as the genre of fantasy itself; it allowed the most unpolished writers—those of the Gothic school, for example—to excuse the irrational. In Lovecraft it is entirely otherwise: Dream is not an artifice; it is a mode of understanding, a means of exploring new worlds.

It is in dreams that Gilman, in "The Dreams in the Witch House," effects his astonishing peregrinations in a multiple-dimensioned universe. It is in dreams that Peaslee relives the experience of his lunatic stay with the Great Race. It is in a dream that the narrator of the "The Shadow over Innsmouth" returns to those of his ancestors who have become Deep Ones. Moreover, dream gives space a supplementary dimension, a depth. Unknown perspectives are opened "beyond the wall of sleep," new spaces are developed where flaming architectures are raised, spaces twirling as if in a kaleidoscope of multiform splendors, resonating with celestial harmonies and displaying landscapes with pure and graceful lines.[12] Dream allows one often to enter an unreal and marvelous "outside," where the few sites that to the dreamer are worthy of being sought, those sites we have loved in youth, are restored and recovered in all their primordial freshness. Because industrial society has so cruelly uprooted us, divorced us from our native soil, and cut off the traditions of the race, so writes Lovecraft,[13] dream is the only means left us to recover our depth and reshape our unity.

But the dreamers whom we have mentioned are only occasional dreamers, who dream almost in spite of themselves; the narrator of "The Shadow over Innsmouth" is at first even frightened by the dreams that convey him to his ancestors, and he needs some time to become accustomed and converted to the new realities they present. It is entirely different with Randolph Carter, who is a *professional dreamer*. From childhood he had rejected his ancestors' faith, bored by the dreary and monotonous solemnity with which the priests tried to transform old myths into terrestrial realities. He doubtless would have remained faithful if religion had been presented to him for what it was: a compendium of picturesque and sonorous rituals, which allowed one temporarily to release emotion but stay in the realm of ethereal fantasy.[14] As for the great modern sorcerers, who have replaced the ancient faith with strange beliefs based on the liberty of man, equality and justice for all, Carter looked upon them with an even more savage hatred. They had uprooted man, taken away his fathers' faith to make him worship equally false deities and adhere to doctrines yet more pernicious than those of yore.[15]

From then on nothing remains for Carter—that is to say, of course, for Lovecraft—but dream. Over the years he has become an unrepentant dreamer, flying off into the most complicated dream-exercises and the most dangerous journeys. When the existence that he leads in Arkham—city of dreams, city of dream—bears down upon him too much, he escapes through nocturnal darkness toward glorious and ancient cities, crosses unreal seas, explores strange and terrible regions. He searches in dream for that supreme beauty, that peace he cannot find on earth, the contact with the divine that the real world refuses him.

The Dream-Quest of Unknown Kadath, which describes in detail the stages of this ardent quest, is a dream epic, an epic of the imagination where Lovecraft reveals his full ability. We meet again the gods of other tales, many monsters, some characters already known to the reader, and especially the same obsessive images. But the universe that is the setting for Carter's singular adventures is situated on the profoundest oneiric level, where horror, though always present, no longer has the unbearable intensity it has in the diurnal tales. All here is attenuated, veiled, shaded: the dreamer in these depths moves easily, with muffled steps.

Thrice had Carter tried, in the course of his dreams, to reach Kadath, the fabulous city. Thrice had he failed; the Gods, hostile to his purpose, had hindered him. But the conquests of the spirit demand perseverance and audacity: behold thus him who once more has renounced the diurnal world; by the same seven hundred steps leading to the Gate of Deeper Slumber does he enter the opaque immensity dream opens for him.

The roads he takes follow the necessarily convoluted tracks of great dream-journeys. He crosses the intricate labyrinth of an enchanted wood, sails from port to port, goes from country to country, crosses mountain after mountain. Without wishing it he often finds himself back at his starting place. The way to supreme truths can only be sinuous, complex, and mystifying. An itinerary fraught with snares, it reminds us of an initiation rite. At each new ordeal, before each new obstacle, the dreamer is compelled to conceive a detour. Or is it that the detour creates the obstacles and determines the ordeal? The dream-process is always inseparable from mythical patterns.

Carter, moreover, engages in his quest only after having at Ulthar consulted the Pnakotic Manuscripts and the *Seven Cryptical Books of Hsan,* where the principal data of the Cthulhu Mythos are consigned. It is these depths of myth the dreamer explores, this myth whose merely sporadic manifestations on the surface are as yet known to us. Is Carter's mad ambition not to attain, beyond the glacial immensity of the terrible desert of Leng, the onyx castle that is the immemorial dwelling of the Old Ones? Is it not the trail of the Gods that he follows, by seeking to recognize divine faces among men, and the traits of that titanic visage carved on the invisible side of Mount Ngranek? And are the ordeals he must overcome not imposed upon him by the very Old Ones for whom he searches, those deities whose name alone, when the characters of the diurnal world invoke them, suffices to give birth to a panic terror . . . ?

The entire tale is organized around the lines defined by the dream-quest, which is also a mythic battle. Sometimes Carter is taken away on board a black galley by the agents of the Other Gods; sometimes he is led on the back of a shantak toward the high-priest of the Outer Ones; sometimes he is precipitated, by the order of Nyarlathotep the "Crawling Chaos," toward black gulfs no dreamer can reach. At every moment he must struggle against Azathoth and his emissaries; and the vicissitudes of this struggle are entirely inscribed within the framework of a well-known mythic structure. In the tales of the Randolph Carter cycle, Lovecraft extends toward the bottom, animates the Cthulhu Mythos *from underneath.* The dreamer *meets* those whom the characters of the surface tales are content merely to *name.*

The images of profound dream also allow the author to erect the map of a myth of whose history he had spoken elsewhere. The reader of *The Dream-Quest of Unknown Kadath* is struck by the geographic precision with which space is constructed. Ulthar, Celephaïs, the sinister gate of Dylath-Leen, Sarkomand, Inganok, and countless other sublime or infamous cities orient the dreamer's quest, that is, materialize it. Thus a mythical topography, where the fabulous places of which the Old Books speak are now localized, is developed by stages around this dream-itinerary. We now know that to attain the abominable Plateau of Leng, a matter dealt with in the *Necronomicon,* we must pass by Ulthar, skirt the

River Skai in the direction of the Southern Sea, and embark at Dylath-Leen for the isle of Oriab where Mount Ngranek rises; then, passing Zar, the region of forgotten dreams, we must reach Celephaïs, in Ooth-Nargai beyond the Tanarian Hills, where Kuranes reigns. We will reach it by following the river Oukranos up to the Cerenarian Sea, after having crossed Kiran and Thran. From Celephaïs, one should sail for the land of Inganok, which is plunged in an eternal half-light; fabulous Kadath is not far. It is raised in the North behind a chain of steep mountains. To be sure, it is easier to go there by air, on the back of a shantak or a night-gaunt from Sarkomand. . . .

Myth commands this organization of space insofar as it materializes a structure of irreversible rapports between Good and Evil, the Sacred and the Sacrilegious. On this map there are zones both divine and demonic. There are luminous cities where crystal palaces tower, and there are gaping pits that communicate with the infernal vaults of Zin. There is Mount Ngranek and the Ultimate Abyss. The space revealed to Carter by the initiates (Atal the Prophet who heard the Gods singing and dancing on the slopes of Mount Hatheg, and Kuranes the monarch who died on earth only to settle into his dream) is an oriented space, where taboos are localized and every step is predetermined.

It is also a space that the vertical axis of the imagination structures powerfully. "To sleep," notes Bachelard, "is to descend and climb like a sentient bottle imp in the waters of the night."[16] Slowly dozing off, Carter first descends the seventy steps leading to the cavern of fire, then the seven hundred steps leading to the Gate of Deeper Slumber. To descend is to begin dreaming; to dream is frequently to descend or fall. Oftentimes it is to have the experience of flying, of soaring, or of a harder ascension. With what effort does Carter scale Mount Ngranek by a wall "which falls straight from unknown heights to unknown depths"![17] Suspended halfway between the summit and the abyss, he progresses with difficulty. But scarcely does he finish climbing and can contemplate the visage of the God carved in the rock than he is attacked by the night-gaunts. The monsters embrace him in their rubbery members and carry him away in a vertiginous plunge toward the lower depths:

> Soon they were plunging hideously downward through inconceivable abysses in a whirling, giddying, sickening rush of dark, tomb-

like air; and Carter felt they were shooting into the ultimate vortex of shrieking and daemoniac madness. He screamed again and again, but whenever he did so the black paws tickled him with greater subtlety. Then he saw a sort of grey phosphorescence about, and guessed they were coming even to that inner world of subterrene horror of which dim legends tell, and which is litten only by the pale death-fires wherewith reeks the ghoulish air and the primal myths of earth's core.[18]

But Carter does not long stay in the Vale of Pnath, land of the enormous bholes;[19] the ghouls of the Upper Worlds of Dream throw down a ladder to him and "for hours he climbed with aching arms and blistered hands. . . ."[20]

To rise, however, does not always demand such exertion from the dreamer. Often the climbing is easy and harmonious, partaking of the rising dynamics of flight. When reading *The Dream-Quest of Unknown Kadath* we are struck by the number of flying monsters enlivening space. Even ships, like the black galley that takes Carter away toward that side of the moon never viewed by men, are relieved of their weight and cavort among the stars. Flights and falls follow one upon the other. After having flown at a considerable height over the Plateau of Leng on the back of a shantak, Carter, fleeing the high-priest dressed in yellow silk, falls into a dark pit: "Of the length of that hideous gliding he could never be sure, but it seemed to take hours of delirious nausea and ecstatic frenzy."[21]

We could almost say that Carter moves more often vertically, in height or in depth, than horizontally. But none of his falls is as impressive, nor as characteristic of dream, as that final fall, when he leaps down from the shantak to escape Nyarlathotep: "Aeons reeled, universes died and were born again, stars became nebulae and nebulae became stars, and still Randolph Carter fell through those endless voids of sentient blackness."[22] Truly, even if myth enriches dream by orienting and shaping it, nevertheless dream gives myth its *profundity*.

The phenomenal originality of Lovecraft lies in this intimate fusion of oneiric vision and mythic elaboration. The end of *The Dream-Quest of Unknown Kadath* is in this regard very revealing: the fantastic tale becomes, in these last pages, a philosophical tale, or apologue. When Carter, accompanied by his grotesque equipage, enters the onyx castle of the Great Old Ones, Nyarlathotep informs him that the latter have deserted their dwelling—*the dwelling which myth had for all eternity assigned them as their residence*—to settle into the marvelous city imagined and sought by the audacious dreamer from Providence.

> All through its palaces of veined marble they revel by day, and when the sun sets they go out in the perfumed gardens and watch the golden glory on temples and colonnades, arched bridges and silver-basined fountains, and wide streets with blossom-laden urns and ivory statues in gleaming rows.[23]

Is Lovecraft trying to tell us that men's dreams are more beautiful than divine reality, to the point of being coveted by the gods? Doubtless; but it is still more interesting to note that myth is dissolved and is reabsorbed, at least partly, in dream. The Great Old Ones, fleeing primordial Kadath, getting out of the Cthulhu Mythos, enter the dream of a man, establish themselves in a city that is the sum, the oneiric totalization of all the cities Carter loved in his youth: Boston, Salem, Providence, Newport, Concord, and many others. Myth not only organizes dream, but is substantially integrated into it.

This amalgamation is important insofar as it at least in part accounts for the profound modifications, beyond an apparent continuity, in the author's behavior toward his own creation. *The Dream-Quest of Unknown Kadath* does not appreciably differ, at least in its constituent elements, from Lovecraft's other tales. The Land of Deeper Slumber, which is underneath the Waking World, also has its monsters, and most hideous ones; we have spoken of them elsewhere. At this deep level of dream, however, some spectacular mutations in the author's repugnances take place. In "Pickman's Model" the metamorphosis of Pickman is presented as a nameless horror. In *The Dream-Quest of Unknown Kadath,* conversely, Carter without displaying exaggerated repugnance associates with the ghouls who, thanks to their leader's mediation, become his allies, his protectors, and somehow even the agents of his ultimate victory over Nyarlathotep. The night-gaunts are similarly transformed into powerful friends. At first they inspire terror, when we learn that they frequently bear off the lava-gatherers to the slopes of Mount Ngranek and that they suck the blood of yaks. Carter himself at first feels only disgust for these faceless monsters with rubbery and prehensile members. And yet, they later render him invaluable services, carrying him over the deserted immensity of the Plateau of Leng to the onyx castle of the Old Ones. As for the zoogs, who meet the dreamer in the vegetable labyrinth of the enchanted wood, they prove, despite their disconcerting aspect, to be useful, serviceable, and of good counsel.

Is this to say that some monsters can be tamed, and that *in these depths* it is possible to come to terms with one's demons? The deities themselves no longer have that horrible aspect, those madness-inducing forms, which characterized them when they manifested themselves in the Waking World. Their progeny in particular—for the gods of the depths willingly borrow human forms—no longer have anything in common with the horror engendered by Lavinia Whateley or with the croaking and viscous abominations of "The Shadow over Innsmouth." On the contrary, their offspring, conceived at random from the frequent visits with which the gods honor humanity, are of an austere and sublime beauty. Nyarlathotep himself is no longer the "Faceless God," or the unclean "flying thing" that he was to be in "The Haunter of the Dark." He appears to Carter with the traits of a seductive young man, arrayed in a scarlet robe and invested with the dignity of an Egyptian god. . . . In the Land of Deeper Slumber it is not only possible to see the gods face to face, but even more to stand up to them; and Carter without too much trouble succeeds in foiling the ultimate ruse of the Crawling Chaos.

This change of attitude toward the divine is even more noticeable in "Through the Gates of the Silver Key."[24] On the other side of the Ultimate Gate, the dreamer finds himself in an unnatural space where the very concept of "dimension" no longer exists. Around him, in a sort of timeless nonspace where the monstrous forms he observes obey no fixed geometric laws, pedestals are raised where veiled silhouettes squat: They are the Great Old Ones whom the author has finally allowed us to meet. But far from being presented as inimical entities, they are now lost in an eternal meditation, far from any dreams of conquest or blasphemous accession to our planet. What is more, they make a place among themselves for the intrepid dreamer.

In "Through the Gates of the Silver Key" the *Necronomicon* is also involved. But the book has lost the horrid notoriety with which Lovecraft had invested it in his Cthulhu Mythos tales: Carter cites a passage where, indeed, the emphasis is on the dangers accompanying the dreamer's enterprises. But it also involves a guide who will come to aid him in crossing the Ultimate Gate. This guide is 'Umr at-Tawil, who has a symbolic name: "The Prolonged-of-Life." We see here the reappearance of the central motif of the Waking World tales, illustrated so hideously by Joseph Curwen and his confreres. But here the prolongation of life is no longer the result of an ignoble vampirism; it is the result of a sort of mystical union—the word is not too strong—with the "All-in-One." Moreover, 'Umr at-Tawil's mission is to prepare Carter for meeting Yog-Sothoth. The ordeal is difficult, and the dreamer experiences ultimate agony when, having attained the final threshold, he loses his identity, or rather, multiplies into an infinity of past, present, future, terrestrial and extraterrestrial Carters. Facing the supreme deity, he can exist only as an "archetype." An ontological horror thus takes hold of the Boston dreamer when he must brutally reintegrate the entity of which only a facet is represented on earth among an infinity of others. But Yog-Sothoth is no longer that archaic and hideous monstrosity elsewhere described; he is, conversely, an immaterial and glorious intelligence who explains life and the world to the reassured and *converted* newcomer. Sacrilege, after all, is only the reverse of the sacred; and Carter, suddenly, rediscovers the Ineffable.

The data of this changing attitude in Lovecraft are not explained by chronology; *The Dream-Quest of Unknown Kadath* was written in the early 1920s, "The Silver Key" in 1926, and "Through the Gates of the Silver Key" in 1932.[25] It is enough to say that the most atrocious of his tales were written before these or at the same time. There is not, we think, a "before" and an "after" in the author's vision of the world; but there is, if we are allowed to use these approximate terms, an "above" and a "below." By this we can better account for the manifest difference in atmosphere between *The Dream-Quest of Unknown Kadath* and, say, "The Dunwich Horror" or "The Shadow over Innsmouth": it is a changing of the oneiric level. We have often hinted at this. Carter, in his interminable quest, moves in the deepest layers of dream, descends the seven hundred steps leading to the Land of Deeper Slumber. The characters of other tales live and act on the surface, in the Waking World. The monsters—*our* monsters—are disquieting, hideous, and execrable only when they leave the thick darkness of our psyche to emerge on the surface of our consciousness. What is intolerable is that we must recognize them as ours. But, some people say, is this not also the only means of detaching them from ourselves?

106

Despite their exceptional oneiric quality, the tales of the Randolph Carter cycle seem less authentically fantastic than the others. We have already affirmed, following the authority of others, that the fantastic exists only where the irrational makes an irruption into the real world. The world in which Carter moves, with its prestigious or sinister cities, its picturesquely named rivers, its ethereal seas that suddenly mingle with the sky, its pleasant or lugubrious landscapes that unfurl to infinity under the earth's surface—this world is not our own. It is a marvelous world, such as Dunsany built in his tales, where the inadmissible has lost its aggressive character because it is manifested in an unreal terrain. What we know of Kadath does not so much recall, despite what the author says, Boston, Providence, or Salem, as Zretazoola found in Sombelenë beyond the Athraminaurean Mountains, or the City of Never, built on the Ultimate Edge of the World: fabulous, luminous, terrible cities, which Sime has delicately drawn in illustrating *The Book of Wonder*. The flying galley, which carries Carter toward the other side of the moon, is that of Loharneth-Lahai, whose hull is made of tight-fitting dreams. The severe and sublime visage carved on Mount Ngranek is that of Ranorada, another god of Pegāna. We are in a closed world, hollow and fragile as a bubble—as one of the bubbles that in another engraving form the dreams of Māna-Yood-Sushāī. The fantastic is, on the contrary, a tear, a disturbance, a transgression, and presupposes a solid, consistent world ruled by immutable laws. The Land of Deeper Slumber belongs no more to reality than does the region at the Edge of the World.

Clearly it belongs to dream; but to a dream experienced as such, before waking, which happens only at the end of a tale. The phenomenon of "distancing," essential to fantastic creation, is not in play here. The basic divorce that must exist between the character's lucidity and the oneiric quality of the images he encounters is not for a moment perceived: Carter is caught in his own dreams.

Thus results an atmosphere of poetic unreality, doubtless seductive, where the author's exuberant imagination designs motifs that, like those of the Irish master, surprise, charm, and arrest the attention. But of the fantastic there is none. Lacking a single reference to the diurnal world, we remain in Wonderland.

Because, by all evidence, writing was for Lovecraft a primitive therapeutic he applied to his phantasms, it would be tempting to ponder the ultimate significance of a dream-journey on such a

level. In the deep waters of dream, the author plays with his demons and somehow refuses to face them. Far from making them
emerge in broad daylight to the surface by the intricate network of
tunnels and pits that vertically shapes his universe, he will join
them in their dark depths. The ghoul no longer makes, as in "The
Outsider," an irruption into a brilliantly lighted room where an
elegant reception is being held; he moves in hoary depths where
he is not perceived as a monster.

Only a professional analyst would know how to interpret con-
vincingly this abortive act of exorcism, this fumbling attempt at a
cure. In general, the psychoanalyst would have much to say about
an oeuvre totally enveloped in dream, and where the pathological
signs of an intimate conflict are clearly betrayed. He would rightly
bring to mind the schizoid personality of the author, fundamentally incapable of establishing a durable contact with reality. He
would presumably put us in touch with the intense horror sexuality inspired in Lovecraft, noting the frequent references in his
work to the "viscous," the "gelatinous," the "flabby," and the
"rubbery." He would invest the images of "tentacles" and "mono-
liths," which recur so insistently under his pen, with a precise
meaning.

But in our decision not to follow this difficult path we plead our
total incompetence. A psychoanalysis of Lovecraft cannot be im-
provised. Moreover, we will not conceal our reservations about
such a necessarily regressive method, which would fix symbols
into an univocal signification and neglect the dynamism of images
that alone are adequate to make psychic activity. Another track is
offered to our inquiry which, we think, will emerge upon less
hazardous perspectives, because it is more rigorously centered on
what is at the heart of our author's work: we will turn our attention
to myth.

10
FROM FABLE TO MYTH

It is in the Cthulhu Mythos that Lovecraft's tales gain their profound unity. Except for some details, all develop the same central theme; all make reference to the same deities; all put on stage the same characters devoted to the same occult practices. Above all, the same images recur under the author's pen with an obsessive insistence, to form a tight web around the mythic contents of the work, ensuring its cohesion and giving it its consistency.

The question we then ask is whether this organized, structured, hierarchical system is a gratuitous fable, a jeu d'esprit, a "cosmic epic" conceived by an idle paranoiac, or whether it involves, at a deep level of consciousness, the most fundamental realities. Did the "old gentleman of Providence" write for the pleasure of writing, as did his "grandfathers"? Or does he convey in his mythic discourse something that might make us seek a more profound interpretation?

Certainly the Cthulhu Mythos is a fable, a pure invention, a fiction. It was elaborated, episode after episode, by the author just

109

as other patient amateurs build houses of cards or put together a jigsaw puzzle. Who could conceivably deny that in a sense it is the disconcerting result of an intense play-activity? The fact is amply demonstrated by an attentive reading of Lovecraft's correspondence. Some of the correspondents or disciples of the dreamer from Providence were even allowed to enter the game, inserting at some point a new deity, or at some other point relating an obscure genealogy. Particularly after the author's death the Cthulhu Mythos became a parlor game—a lucrative game, to be sure, taken over for commercial ends by publishers and movie producers. . . . *This* myth—need we say so?—interests us not at all. But through the data of the fable (the data, at least, established by Lovecraft) there is outlined a movement of return toward the fundamental, the initial, the exemplary. Under the surface of the narrative, which necessarily follows the thread of an articulated discourse, can confusedly be perceived structures reminiscent of the great myths that have nourished humanity and that seem to have been *inherited* rather than invented. For all the clouding by a profusion of horrible or grotesque details, the general schema—the "pattern," as the mythologists say—of the Cthulhu Mythos is this return to the beginning, the source, the "principle of life."

If we are to believe the most respected commentators, the essential of myth is to remind man of the times signifying the beginnings, the Great Time at the beginning of time. All myth is *myth of origins,* and under one form or another tells the tale of Creation. It tells of the first Act, it recounts what happened in the times when something could happen, *in illo tempore,* in the times of the gods and the exemplary beings who existed at the birth of our planet.

"Myth," writes Mircea Eliade, "tells a sacred history; it relates an advent which has taken place in primordial times, the fabulous times of the beginnings. In other words, myth tells how, thanks to the exploits of Supernatural Beings, a reality has come into existence."[1]

How, then, can we *not* think of the imaginary voyages Lovecraft undertakes vicariously, through his characters, toward the most hidden eras of history? How can we not recall, more precisely, the adventures Peaslee knew in the "shadow out of time," among the Great Race, hundreds of millions of years before the appearance of man on earth?

Things of inconceivable shape, [the myths] implied, had reared towers to the sky and delved into every secret of Nature before the first

110

amphibian forbear of man had crawled out of the hot sea three hundred million years ago. Some had come down from the stars; a few were as old as the cosmos itself; others had arisen swiftly from terrene germs as far behind the first germs of our life cycle as those germs are behind ourselves. Spans of thousands of millions of years, and linkages with other galaxies and universes, were spoken of. Indeed, there was no such thing as time in its humanly accepted sense.[2]

Of little importance here are the artifices used by the author to send his character back to this fabulous epoch of history. What counts is that Peaslee breaks for a while with secular time and reintegrates himself with primordial time, the intense time of the beginnings. Projected out of ordinary temporality, he becomes— literally—the contemporary of legendary beings. He is called upon to live the events the memory of which the human race has lost, to participate in that initial fullness Mircea Eliade tells us is the chance for the sick man—and perhaps for Lovecraft?—to recover his strength: "The function of myth is not to *conserve* the remembrance of the primordial event, but to *project* the sick man *to where that event is in the process of occurring*, i.e. to the dawn of Time, the beginning."

Later on we will see what conclusions concerning the author can be drawn about this *therapeutic* significance of mythic behavior. For the moment let us note that the same method is found in many other tales and particularly in *At the Mountains of Madness*. The survivors of the Pabodie expedition become provisionally the "contemporaries" of the Great Old Ones and of . . . a shoggoth. In contrast with the preceding tale, the artifice here consists in reanimating the fabulous beings right in secular time. But the result is the same: humans suddenly find themselves confronted with entities who were, as we are made to understand in the course of the tale, *models*. In the Cthulhu Mythos, everything rests on the belief that in prodigiously obscure times, primordial deities from the stars—all myth necessarily having a cosmic dimension— were installed on the earth, and by their arrival began earth life. This is the tale told by the frescoes painted on the walls of the subterranean tunnels explored by the narrator and his companion in the ruins of that ancient city on the malefic Plateau of Leng. These "astral beings" are, par excellence, the actors of a primordial drama played *at the beginning*. And to illustrate this drama, we need only recall the terrible struggle between the Old Ones and the Great Race, a fight whose echoes can here or there be perceived, or again the rebellion of these premier deities from the other gods, and their ultimate chastisement.[3] In each tale the time of the story is always defined by reference to mythic times, which is the Time of Cthulhu. The characters, by will or accident, leave chronological time to recover the sacred—or sacrilegious?—time of the beginning. In this context is it not significant that Randolph Carter, in the last pages of "Through the Gates of the Silver Key," suddenly disappears from the room he is in by entering a clock? We can suppose that he has returned, beyond cosmic space, to faraway Yaddith, where time is qualitatively other than that which it is on earth.

It is certainly patently significant that in "The Silver Key" Carter's mythic quest, which will put him in the presence of Yog-Sothoth himself, coincides with the quest for the images of his childhood. Having, at age fifty, made the tour of human vanities, he decides to go to the old family home, obeying the suggestions of a strange dream, and becomes again the child "Randy" that he was forty years before. He becomes so in the literal sense: familiar voices surround him again, and it is a youngster in knee breeches and smock who applies the "silver key" to the lock of the Ultimate Gate.

Here the return to origins is made in the framework of an individual psyche. Randolph Carter becomes, in the most literal sense of the term, the contemporary of his first childhood; he is projected, by the author's own wish, to the beginning of his personal history. He is reinstated in the "beatific" period, the "paradisiacal" time of the beginnings, breaking with the sterile and chronological time of the adult world he had regrettably entered. Again, the psychoanalyst would have much to say about this oneiric regression to the initial stage of the individual psyche. We will leave to others better prepared than ourselves the task of doing this. Let us restrain ourselves and show, for our part, that the mythic approach coincides once again with the oneiric experience. Carter reattains childhood, comes back to the initial stage of his existence, and by this rediscovers the fundamental truths that in the beginning presided over the development of worlds. The silver key is the symbol for the time of infancy, which permits Carter to attain the infancy of Time.

Placing them in this context, we can better understand the "genealogical" quests in which many of the characters indulge. These beings who examine the archives of their ancestral dwellings, who comb attics in search of old familial correspondence, or who watch for the least clue capable of clearing up the past of their "stock" in effect illustrate this same "myth of origins." The importance accorded by some of them to the "line," to the "ancients," testifies to their wish to reproduce *in their time* what took place *at the beginning of Time*. To achieve this, they use ritual, which, as is well known, has no other function than the reactualization of myth. We think of all those ceremonies we have elsewhere recalled, the aim of which is the awakening of the Great Old Ones and their return to our planet. What do the worshippers of Dagon, Cthulhu, and Yog-Sothoth seek if not to repeat archaic actions to make history repeat itself, the fabulous history of the time when R'lyeh emerged from the waves . . . ? What we were saying earlier about the metamorphosis of language during these strange rites takes on a new significance: Lovecraft, conscious of the demands of myth, abolished lay, ordinary language for the duration of these ceremonies and substituted a language—sacred, secret—which he re-created. Yog-Sothoth must not be addressed in everyday language; one cannot hope to communicate with him but by using formulas known only to initiates and priests. The ritualistic re-creation of the world requires the institution of a new Word.

The cosmic dimension of the Lovecraftian universe again testifies to its ties with myth. The space in his tales is an *astral space,* which extends to the very confines of the universe, beyond the "Edge of the World." The planet Yaddith, where Carter spends several million years in the body of the sorcerer Zkauba, whose aspect it is best to hide; the planet Yuggoth, whence those strange crustacean-shelled creatures came; the star Vega, toward which Nyarlathotep steers the shantak mounted by Carter; and many other stars that shine in the skies of . . . Providence indicate not the limits of Lovecraft's mythic universe, but the directions to which it ceaselessly extends. Lovecraft, reactualizing cosmogonic myth, re-creates the cosmos. Returning to the beginning of Time, he distributes the worlds in space, taking care, however, to reserve a place for Chaos, over which a blind and idiot god rules. . . .

We may perhaps be puzzled by the apparently close correspondence between the Cthulhu Mythos and the "real" myths of humanity, such as those presented us in the most recent and pertinent studies. It will be still simpler to find in the Lovecraftian universe the constituent elements of the closer and more familiar myths of Greco-Roman antiquity, such as the revolt of certain gods, their chastisement, their imprisonment. And yet, to explain the presence of Hypnos, Neptune, Hermes, or Zeus in such-and-such a tale, it is not enough to recall the author's perfect knowledge of classical mythology. Nor does the fact that he had read Frazer, Fiske, and so many other mythologists whom he cites in his letters the more imply that the Cthulhu Mythos was solely an abstract, rational construction, an ersatz myth articulated by logical thought; at least it does not imply exclusively this. Certainly the Cthulhu Mythos has been elaborated from a structure common to all myths. We admit that it was elaborated as a game, the game of a neurotic and idle scholar.

But may we not believe that Lovecraft, insofar as he *dreamed* a feigned mythology, restored to it its value as myth as well as its primordial irrationality? Dreaming at first within acquired structures, he rediscovered in his unconscious—or at a profound level of consciousness—inherited structures. By dream he reanimated petrified schemas; in dream he passed from fable to myth, or better, from fable he redid a myth. Need we thus be astonished? In a world that like our own has banished the irrational, the dark zones of the psyche were the last refuge of myth. "Dream is a cosmogony of the night. Every night, the dreamer builds the world anew."[4] This lovely formula of Bachelard's better defines Lovecraft's method than we have done, mythic and oneiric at one and the same time, or mythic *because* it is oneiric.

We thus return to our first remark, concerning the profound, *therapeutic* significance of myth. Lovecraft's tales can be read, as we have said, as the journal of a treatment. It is now possible, in the context we have just advanced, to be a little more precise. What seems fundamental in his work is this oneiric regression into the heart of a mythic structure, into the fullness of primordial times, which is also the time of childhood. For Lovecraft as for all other mythographers, the beginning is the model, the perfection. Parenthetically, let us here refer to what we said earlier about distinguishing Lovecraft's tales from those of science fiction. According to him, science and intelligence were at the beginning of time. Then men forgot, and the human race degenerated. . . . Here again is an important aspect of mythic behavior, this notion of decadence from high times, from times signifying the beginning, an aspect that, as we have seen, occupies an important place in the author's *Weltanshauung*. There would doubtless be much to say about the rapports that existed in him between racism and mythic thought,[5] and his "fascism" could in part be explained by this return to the "myth of origins." By what other means could he fight against the degeneracy of his contemporaries, if not to return to the source and praise the former purity of the race? But this is a secondary aspect of a fundamental question. It is essential to see how the "myth of origins," through the transfer it makes to the intense time of the beginnings, re-creates life and allows the sick man to participate in the fullness of creation. It is, as Mircea Eliade tells us, a remedy for all "critical and existential situations where man is driven to hopelessness."[6]

Lovecraft was, as we have seen, a man without hope. Unstable, sick, unhappy, obstinately rejecting what he considered the delusions of faith, fed on nihilistic philosophies, he had frequently thought of suicide. Only his dreams—his correspondence testifies to it—permitted him to overcome each crisis and to try once again to live. Did he not in dream find, in the blackest moments, the unexpected help of secret and vitalizing forces?

We are then tempted to regard the Cthulhu Mythos, whose elaboration was slow, progressive, and continuous, as the adequate receptacle for the author's anguish, where, in the waters of dream, it could "precipitate," form deposits in precise, horrible, *monstrous* shapes at the bottom of a structure ready to receive them and give them meaning.

Driven by a myth—a necessarily *oriented* structure, based on the quest for and the revelation of the sacred—horror can only be expressed by and in sacrilege: the impious cults, hideous ceremonies, blasphemous rites elsewhere mentioned, which tell a reverse history of salvation. It is at this deep level that the cure operates: because the sick man recognizes these images of horror as his own, he is in a position to assume them fully and thereby overcome them. To give a material representation to anguish is in itself to be freed from it. To formulate sacrilege is somehow to recover the meaning of the sacred, even if, as was probably so with Lovecraft, it is basically a playful representation. For we can never totally invent our monsters; they express our inner selves too much for that. Game is part of the search for a cure, as fable is a step toward myth.

CONCLUSION

It would be an exaggeration to make Lovecraft another Poe: Lovecraft had irritating naïvetés, verbal excesses, unpleasant political opinions. In some ways he was frankly puerile; his excessive love of cats made him write several lovely pages, but also led him to conceive, in *The Dream-Quest of Unknown Kadath,* an episode quite grotesque. His veneration of Machen and Dunsany often betrayed him; in many tales we find too faithful echoes of his mentors. The American critic Edmund Wilson said of his work that the only real horror to be found there was that of bad taste and execrable art.[1] Without sharing this severe opinion, we must admit that Poe's art is of an entirely different quality. It belongs forever to the realm of universal literature.

In, however, the strictly fantastic realm, Daniel George's judgment is itself not unfitting. "Compared to his tales," he has written, "Poe resembles chamber music." In fact, the disciple often surpassed the master in the analysis and description of the horrible and the blasphemous. And the Cthulhu Mythos gives Lovecraft's

117

work a unity, a depth that Poe's lacks. Let us remember that our purpose was to add this brief study to the file of a precise genre. In the context of weird literature, and in that context alone, the work of our author takes on a relief and an importance. It allows us, it seems, to formulate conclusive remarks about the fantastic, which, without being at all dogmatic or normative, could perhaps help us the better to understand or savor similar works.

First of all, Lovecraft's tales unequivocally bring to light the connection between the fantastic and the oneiric. To judge by his example, the writing of a fantastic tale consists in substituting nocturnal images for the clear images that directly signify diurnal life: dark images, in the material sense of the term, fraught with the characteristic symbols of dream. Thus are the images of the labyrinths, spiral staircases, black gulfs, putrid waters, and closed spaces explained, and thus ought they to be read: images which constitute a vocabulary of anguish and which, if we believe in the universality of the structures of the imagination, ensure what we can call an "intense communication" between the author and his readers, a communication "through the depths."

But it is at the same time important, as we have seen, that the characters who encounter these dream-images be lucid, conscious. The fantastic necessarily implies the presence, at the thickest level of dream, of a conscious intelligence. Indeed, the fantastic is born, more precisely, at the very instant the author *becomes aware* of his dream-images, "reifies" them, and detaches himself from them, not without having placed the hero, whose premier function is to prolong his awareness, in this impossible and "real" world. Let us remember here what we said at the beginning of this book: many clues allow us to understand that, in most of Lovecraft's tales, the main character—whether his name be Charles Dexter Ward, Edward Derby, Olney, Malone, or simply "I"—*is* the author. It is his glance that perceives the horror, the split, the transgression; it is in his glance that terror is born.

This should allow us to refine our appreciation of the apparent relation of the fantastic to the pathological. To be sure, the fantastic is fostered by the disturbances introduced by neurosis, insofar as they accentuate the chaotic aspect of dream, amplify anguish, and are made manifest by the persistence of dream-images at the level of wakefulness. But it is as clear that no work can properly be classified as fantastic through which the author has not "recovered" and recognized these images for his own. Lacking such an identification, he remains the prisoner of his delirium, the oeuvre remaining mad, savage, alienated. We are told that the pictures drawn and the tales written by madmen are sometimes beautiful, but they do not belong to the fantastic: lacking is a clear way of looking at things, indispensable to create "distance" and perspective. The emergence of fantastic art is conditioned by the author's mastery of his phantasms, whence the primordial importance of a *cure*, of which we have spoken before, and which we consider an absolute prerequisite. The writer of fantasy ought also to *want* to create fear, and this is derived directly from a cure. There must be a purpose, a deliberate intention to communicate anguish. Here technique takes over, arranging and making hierarchical the unrefined data of dream. It organizes suspense, it introduces the irrational into the heart of a causal series, it condenses the dream around a plot. All tales of fantasy are an articulated, dramatized dream. Their quality depends in large part on the working of a finely geared mechanism, which must run without hitches. But technique ought always to remain subservient to dream.

What Lovecraft teaches us, and what he himself learned from Machen,[2] is that the best fantasy is that which is rooted in folklore, tradition, and myth. Puritanism and the history of New England play the same role in our author's tales as medieval myth did in the Gothic novels of the end of the eighteenth century. Somehow, myth, in the superficial sense of the term, orients and localizes dream-activity, thereby assuring it an even greater intensity and benefic homogeneity.

On a personal level, myth gives depth and efficiency to the fantastic, precisely insofar as this return to the primordial it involves coincides with a quest for a cure, and also because it permits the irrational to be built on the foundations of the universal psyche. At the most, the idea would be defensible that anything truly fantastic implies a return to *archetypes*.

It will always be impossible to define the fantastic universally, which is too rich, too basic to be encompassed definitively by any discourse. Examples, complementary or contradictory, can but illustrate that Lovecraft's work is one, a very significant one, we believe, and particularly if we consider the time and place in which he lived.

He vehemently stood, in his letters, against the ravages of industrial civilization, which was attacking man at his deepest level: isolating him from the past, from the traditions of his race, tearing him from his native soil; in a word, alienating him. From this viewpoint, fantastic creation is a protest and a refusal. No; life is not as simple, rudimentary, and facile as the billboard advertisements might lead us to believe. No; the laws that rule the universe are not as well known as popular science—the only type of science possible in a "democratic" society, based on numbers—seems to indicate. No; space is not as certain, time is not as "chronological," the past is not as dead as some people declare. In truth, there are more things in heaven and *under the earth* than are dreamt of in our philosophies.

In a society that is becoming each day more anesthetized and repressive, the fantastic is at once an evasion and the mobilization of anguish. It restores man's sense of the sacred or the sacrilegious; it above all gives back to him his lost depth. For the myth of the automobile, the washing machine, and the vacuum cleaner, for the modern myths of the new world that are merely surface myths, Lovecraft substituted the Cthulhu Mythos.

ABBREVIATIONS

Dagon	*Dagon and Other Macabre Tales* (1986)
Dark Brotherhood	*The Dark Brotherhood and Other Pieces* (1966)
Dunwich Horror	*The Dunwich Horror and Others* (1984)
JHL	John Hay Library, Brown University, Providence, R.I.
Mountains of Madness	*At the Mountains of Madness and Other Novels* (1985)
SL	*Selected Letters* (1965–76; 5 vols.)

NOTES

Author's Preface

1. [Much of this "critical apparatus" has been restored in this translation; see Translator's Preface.]

Introduction

1. [A reference to Lévy's article, "Fascisme et fantastique, ou le cas Lovecraft."]

2. [The first two volumes of *Selected Letters* appeared from Arkham House in 1965 and 1968; the third came out in 1971, and the fourth and fifth in 1976.]

3. [The biography did come out: L. Sprague de Camp's *Lovecraft: A Biography* (1975). It has, however, not been generally accepted as either an accurate or impartial account of Lovecraft's life and work.]

4. [See, for example, T. Todorov, *Introduction à la littérature fantastique* (1970; Eng. tr. 1973); E. Rabkin, *The Fantastic in Literature* (1976).]

5. [Modern scholars now refer to Lovecraft's myth-cycle merely as the Lovecraft Mythos; see my *Reader's Guide to H. P. Lovecraft* (1982), chap. 5.]

6. [Derleth and Donald Wandrei founded Arkham House in 1939 by publishing Lovecraft's legendary *The Outsider and Others*, in 1,268 copies. Arkham House print runs rarely exceed 3,000 copies, but the recent Lovecraft fiction volumes—*The Dunwich Horror and Others, At the Mountains of Madness and Other Novels*, and *Dagon and Other Macabre Tales*—are being kept in print by Arkham House and copies of them now surpass 10,000. Lévy was writing some time before the major paperback publications of Lovecraft, by Beagle/Ballantine Books in the United States and Panther Books in England, got underway in 1969, which have disseminated hundreds of thousands of copies of Lovecraft's fiction.]

7. [This was "Hypnos" (*Planète*, 1 [Oct.–Nov. 1961], 47–51), which was prefaced by the celebrated article by Bergier, "Lovecraft, ce grand génie venu d'ailleurs" (pp. 43–46).]

8. [See note 7. The article was a revised version of the introduction to the first volume of Lovecraft in French, *La Couléur tombée du ciel* (1954).]

9. [A tendency still evident in the most recent memoirs, those of H. Warner Munn (*Whispers*, Dec. 1976) and Vrest Orton (*Whispers*, Mar. 1982).]

10. [*L'Herne*'s twelfth issue (1969) was entirely devoted to Lovecraft. It did not include all or even many of the better American studies; most were taken from *The Dark Brotherhood and Other Pieces*.]

11. See George G. Raddin, *An Early New York Library of Fiction* (New York: H. W. Wilson Co., 1940).

12. In the preface to *The Algerine Captives* (1797), Royal Tyler, a little-known American writer, speaks of a dairymaid, Dolly, and a laborer, Jonathan, who "amused themselves into so agreeable a terrour with the haunted houses and hobgoblins of Mrs. Ratcliffe that they were both afraid to sleep alone." See "Preface to Three XVIIIth Century Novels," in *The Algerine Captives* (Los Angeles: Augustan Reprint Society, 1957), ix.

13. See the unpublished list of the readings of Mme. de Rieux at the Virginia Historical Society in Richmond, where, of the several thousand novels read by her from 1806 to 1823, close to 200 are Gothic novels.

14. *The Abbess* (Baltimore: S. Sower & J. W. Butler, 1801). The copy consulted can be found in the New York Society Library.

15. "One merit the writer may at least claim, that of calling forth the passions and engaging the sympathy of the reader by means hitherto unemployed by preceding authors. Puerile superstition and exploded manners, Gothic castles and chimeras, are the materials usually employed for this end. The incidents of Indian hostility, and the perils of the Western wilderness, are far more suitable; and for a native of America to overlook these would admit of no apology." Charles Brockden Brown, *Edgar Huntly*, ed. David Lee Clark (New York, 1928), xxiii.

16. [Vol. 7 of the *Collected Works of Ambrose Bierce* (1909–12; rpt. New York: Gordian Press, 1966). See also *The Enlarged Devil's Dictionary*, ed. E. J. Hopkins (Garden City, N.Y.: Doubleday & Co., 1967).]

17. [James's horror tales have been collected in *The Ghostly Tales of Henry James*, ed. Leon Edel (New Brunswick: Rutgers University Press, 1948; New York: Grosset & Dunlap, 1963).]

18. [See *Wandering Ghosts* (1911). See also Crawford's novels, *The Witch of Prague, Khaled*, and *Zoroaster*.]

19. [*The King in Yellow* (1895; rpt. Freeport, N.Y.: Books for Libraries Press, 1969). Also of note is *In Search of the Unknown* (1904; rpt. Westport, Conn.: Hyperion Press, 1974) and *The Mystery of Choice* (1897; rpt. Freeport, N.Y.: Books for Libraries Press, 1969).]

20. [*The Wind in the Rose-Bush* (1903; rpt. New York: Garnett Press, 1969). In 1974 Arkham House issued *The Collected Ghost Stories of Mary E. Wilkins-Freeman*.]

1: The Outsider

1. Lovecraft to J. F. Morton, 14 Mar. 1924 (SL I.327).
2. "[My] ancestry was that of unmixed English gentry"; see Lovecraft to Edwin Baird, 3 Feb. 1924 (SL I.296).
3. See Lovecraft to F. B. Long, Nov. 1927 (SL II.181).
4. See Lovecraft to M. W. Moe, 8 Dec. 1914 (SL I.6).
5. See Lovecraft, *Some Notes on a Nonentity*, 9.
6. Ibid.
7. [Fifty-four issues, produced weekly from 2 Aug. 1903 to Jan. 1906, survive, with sixteen more from then to Feb. 1909. More were undoubtedly written, but they have not been preserved.]
8. [Lovecraft published monthly articles in the *Pawtuxet Valley Gleaner* (Phenix, R.I.) from July to Dec. 1906 (and possibly 1907 and 1908), and in the *Providence Tribune*, morning, evening, and Sunday editions, from Aug. 1906 to June 1908. Later he had articles in the *Providence Evening News* (1914–18) and the *Asheville* [N.C.] *Gazette-News* (1915).]
9. Lovecraft to M. W. Moe, 8 Dec. 1914 (SL I.7).
10. Here is how Lovecraft defined it himself: "one of several nation-wide correspondence organizations of literary novices who publish papers of their own and form collectively a miniature world of helpful, mutual criticism and encouragement." *Some Notes on a Nonentity*, 12.
11. Lovecraft explains the complicated mechanism of this group in a letter to Kleiner, 4 June 1916 (SL I.23).
12. [Note Lovecraft's remark in "The Defence Remains Open!" (1921): "There are probably seven persons, in all, who really like my work; and they are enough." *In Defence of Dagon*, 21.]
13. See *In Defence of Dagon*.—M.L., S.T.J.
14. [Lovecraft was president of the U.A.P.A. from July 1917 to July 1918, although he was official editor for much of the period between 1920 and 1925. He had been vice president in 1915–16.]
15. See Lovecraft to M. W. Moe, 18 May 1922 (SL I.179).
16. [This assertion is denied by R. Alain Everts in "Howard Phillips Lovecraft and Sex: Or the Sex Life of a Gentleman."]
17. Lovecraft to C. A. Smith, 18 Feb. 1927 (SL II.103).
18. [Lovecraft did not write for the short-lived *Home Brew* after the appearance of "The Lurking Fear" there in 1923.]
19. See Lovecraft to V. Starrett, 11 Apr. 1927 (SL II.124).
20. See Lovecraft to B. A. Dwyer, June 1927 (SL II.139).
21. [The actual divorce proceedings were carried out in 1929, but the final decree was never signed.]
22. See Lovecraft to Mrs. F. C. Clark, 2 May 1929 (ms., JHL).
23. Ibid.
24. [See "The Cats of Ulthar," "The Rats in the Walls," and esp. *The Dream-Quest of Unknown Kadath*.]
25. [To be exact, forty-six years and seven months.]
26. "Lovecraft in Providence," 124.
27. Lovecraft to F. B. Long, 24 July 1923 (SL I.239).
28. "At night, when the objective world has slunk back into its cavern & left dreamers to their own, there come inspirations & capabilities impossible at any less magical & quiet hour. No one knows whether or not he is a writer unless he has tried writing at night." Lovecraft to Mrs. F. C. Clark, 1 Sept. 1925 (MS., JHL).

29. "What I am, is a hater of actuality"; Lovecraft to F. B. Long, 13 May 1923 (SL I.229). [But the rest of Lovecraft's remarks is also highly significant in terms of his aesthetic theory: "—an enemy to time and space, law and necessity. I crave a world of gorgeous and gigantic mystery, splendour, and terror, in which reigns no limitation save that of the untrammelled imagination. Physical life and experience, with the narrowings of artistic vision they create in the majority, are the objects of my most profound contempt. . . . My loathing is not from the standpoint of Puritan morality, but from that of aesthetic independence—I revolt at the notion that physical life is of any value or significance."]

30. See Lovecraft to J. F. Morton, 29 May 1923 (SL I.232).

31. See Lovecraft to R. Kleiner, 23 Jan. 1920 (SL I.106–7).

32. Lovecraft to R. Kleiner, 23 Apr. 1921 (SL I.129).

33. Lovecraft to Long, 8 Jan. 1924 (SL I.283).

34. Lovecraft to Long, 7 Feb. 1924 (SL I.305).

35. See Lovecraft to Long, 3 June 1923 and 4 Sept. 1923 (SL I.233, 248).

36. Sonia H. Davis, *The Private Life of H. P. Lovecraft*, 19.—M.L., S.T.J.

37. Lovecraft to F. B. Long, 13 May 1923 (SL I.227).

38. [The actual phrase is "brutality of the ancient Teutonic sort"; see Lovecraft to R. Kleiner, 23 Dec. 1917 (SL I.53).]

39. "Editorial," *Conservative*, 1, no. 2 (July 1915).

40. [See Lovecraft to Kleiner, 4 June 1916 (SL I.23); "Old England and the Hyphen," *Conservative*, 2, no. 3 (October 1916); "Department of Public Criticism," *United Amateur*, July 1917.]

41. "In a Major Key," *Conservative*, July 1915.

42. See "Bolshevism," *Conservative*, July 1919.

43. Lovecraft to Morton, 10 Feb. 1923 (SL I.207f.).

44. See Sonia H. Davis, *Private Life*, 23. L. Sprague de Camp (*Lovecraft: A Biography*, 466) believes that, since the first English translation of *Mein Kampf* was published only in 1933, a year after Lovecraft's last meeting with his wife, she could not have known about his reading the volume. She could, however, have heard about it indirectly, e.g. through correspondence with Lovecraft's associates.—M.L., S.T.J.

45. Lovecraft to Morton, 10 Feb. 1923 (SL I.209).

46. "De Triumpho Naturae: The Triumph of Nature over Northern Ignorance," included in *Juvenilia: 1897–1905*, 36–37.—M.L., S.T.J.

47. "On the Creation of Niggers," included in *Saturnalia and Other Poems*, 1.—M.L., S.T.J.

48. See Lovecraft to Annie E. P. Gamwell, 26 Feb. 1925 (ms., JHL).

49. Lovecraft to Mrs. F. C. Clark, 13 July 1925 (ms., JHL).

50. Lovecraft to the Gallomo, 30 Sept. 1919 (SL I.90).

51. Lovecraft to M. W. Moe, 19 May 1922 (SL I.181).

52. Lovecraft to Long, 21 Mar. [1924] (SL I.333–34).

53. See Lovecraft to Long, 21 Aug. 1926 (SL II.64–69).

54. Lovecraft to R. Kleiner, 25 Nov. 1915 (SL I.17).

55. Lovecraft to the Gallomo, 6 Oct. 1921 (SL I.156).

56. Lovecraft to Mrs. F. C. Clark, 6 July 1925 (ms., JHL).

57. Lovecraft to Zealia Bishop, 13 Feb. 1928 (SL II.226).

58. "Nothing really amounts to anything"; Lovecraft to Long, 8 Jan. 1924 (SL I.284).

59. Lovecraft to Moe, 16 Jan. 1915 (SL I.10).

60. Lovecraft to the Kleicomolo, Oct. 1916 (SL I.28).

61. Lovecraft to M. W. Moe, 15 May 1918 (SL I.60).

62. Lovecraft to B. A. Dwyer, 26 Mar. 1927 (SL II.119).

63. Lovecraft to Long, 20 Feb. 1929 (SL II.269–71).

64. Lovecraft to R. Kleiner, 23 Feb. 1918 and 14 Sept. 1919 (SL I.56–57, 86f.).

65. Lovecraft to R. Kleiner, 13 May 1921 (SL I.132).
66. Lovecraft to Long, 20 Feb. 1929 (SL II.261f.).
67. Lovecraft to Zealia Bishop, 13 Feb. 1928 (SL II.227f.).
68. Lovecraft to the Kleicomolo, Oct. 1916 (SL I.26).
69. Lovecraft to F. B. Long, 6 Sept. 1927 (SL II.165).
70. [See, e.g., Lovecraft to D. Wandrei, 19 Jan. 1928 (SL II.222).]
71. "When I write stories, Edgar Allan Poe is my model"; see Lovecraft to R. Kleiner, 20 Jan. 1916 (SL I.19). "Poe was my God of Fiction"; Lovecraft to R. Kleiner, 2 Feb. 1916 (SL I.20).
72. "To me Poe is the apex of fantastic art"; Lovecraft to F. B. Long, 3 May 1922 (SL I.173).
73. [See the facsimile of Lovecraft to R. Kleiner, 31 Mar. 1920, facing p. 91 of SL I.]
74. Lovecraft to C. A. Smith, 30 July 1923 (SL I.243).
75. "Supernatural Horror in Literature," first published in *Recluse* (1927), then serially in slightly revised form in *Fantasy Fan* (Oct. 1933–Feb. 1935). First complete publication of the revised text in *The Outsider and Others* (1939).—M.L., S.T.J.
76. Lovecraft to F. B. Long, 6 Apr. 1923 (SL I.216).
77. Lovecraft to E. Toldridge, 8 Mar. 1929 (SL II.315). [The printed text errs in reading "my Lovecraft pieces."]
78. Lovecraft to Zealia Bishop, 28 Aug. 1927 (SL II.160).
79. See Lovecraft to [W.] Harris, 25 Feb.–1 Mar. 1929 (SL II.300f.).

2: Dwellings and Landscapes

1. Lovecraft to Zealia Bishop, 13 Feb. 1928 (SL II.229).
2. "That ethereal sense of identity with my own native & hereditary soil & institutions is the one essential condition of intellectual life—& even of a sense of complete existence & waking reality—which I cannot do without. Like Antaeus of old, my strength depends on repeated contact with the soil of the Mother Earth that bore me." Lovecraft to C. A. Smith, 15 Oct. 1927 (SL II.177).
3. "New York . . . has no central identity or meaning, & no clean-cut relationship either to its own past or to anything else in particular." Lovecraft to D. Wandrei, 10 Feb. 1927 (SL II.100).
4. See an unpublished letter to Mrs. F. C. Clark, 12 June 1930: "Landscapes like this have a deeply ingrained character, & exude a positive kind of antiquity. To enter one is almost like walking at will through time and space, or climbing bodily into some strange picture on the wall. I disagree with that Distaff article . . . in which it is stated that the New England landscapes lack the element of the weird and the macabre. To me, they possess it as no other landscape does. Only in New England do I feel that odd undercurrent of sinister and unholy life in the brooding fields and woods, & the little huddled farmhouses. Elsewhere I find *antiquity*, but never *concealed terror*. Terror is the legacy of a long Puritan heritage with its unnatural philosophy—the heritage of Salem, Endicott, & the Mathers—and only those visible symbols closely connected with this system possess the terror element to a complete degree." Ms., JHL.—M.L., S.T.J.
5. "It was too much like a landscape of Salvator Rosa; too much like some forbidden woodcut in a tale of terror." See "The Colour out of Space," in *Dunwich Horror*, 54.
6. "The Lurking Fear."
7. "The Strange High House in the Mist."
8. [See, e.g., Lovecraft to M. W. Moe, 4 Sept. 1923 (SL I.245).]

9. See Lovecraft to Anne T. Renshaw, 14 June 1922; to Mrs. F. C. Clark, 29 Sept. 1922 (SL I.187, 198).
10. [*The Case of Charles Dexter Ward.*]
11. "Herbert West—Reanimator."
12. See "The Hound," in *Dagon*, 172.
13. "Dagon."
14. "The Temple."
15. *The Dream-Quest of Unknown Kadath.*
16. "The Call of Cthulhu," in *Dunwich Horror*, 150.
17. *Dagon*, 266.

3: The Metamorphoses of Space

1. In *Mountains of Madness*, 441.
2. "Garish daylight shewed only squalor and alienage and the noxious elephantiasis of climbing, spreading stone where the moon had hinted of loveliness and elder magic; and the throngs of people that seethed through the flume-like streets were squat, swarthy strangers with hardened faces and narrow eyes, shrewd strangers without dreams and without kinship to the scenes around them. . . . Upon making this discovery I ceased to sleep comfortably; though something of resigned tranquillity came back as I gradually formed the habit of keeping off the streets by day and venturing abroad only at night, when darkness calls forth what little of the past still hovers wraith-like about. . . ." See "He," in *Dagon*, 267.
3. "We squeezed through interstices, tiptoed through corridors, clambered over brick walls, and once crawled on hands and knees through a low, arched passage of stone whose immense length and tortuous twistings effaced at last every hint of geographical location I had managed to preserve." Ibid., 269.
4. [*Dagon*, 209.]
5. [This quotation was first cited by Jacques Bergier, who in "Lovecraft, ce grand génie venu d'ailleurs" wrote that Lovecraft had so replied when Bergier had asked him in a letter how he had managed so faithfully to capture the French atmosphere of the tale. There is some question whether Bergier thus actually corresponded with Lovecraft, and the quotation may be apocryphal.]
6. *Dunwich Horror*, 84.
7. ["Hypnos."]
8. ["The Dreams in the Witch House."]
9. "My cynicism and scepticism are increasing, and from an entirely new cause—the Einstein theory. The latest eclipse observations seem to place this system among the facts which cannot be dismissed, and assumedly it removes the last hold which reality or the universe can have on the independent mind. All is chance, accident, and ephemeral illusion—a fly may be greater than Arcturus, and Durfee Hill may surpass Mount Everest—assuming them to be removed from the present planet and differently environed in the continuum of space-time. There are no values in all infinity—the least idea that there are is the supreme mockery of all. All the cosmos is a jest, and fit to be treated only as a jest, and one thing is as true as another. I believe everything and nothing—for all is chaos, always has been, and always will be." Lovecraft to James F. Morton, 26 May 1923 (SL I.231).
10. See Pauwels and Bergier, *Le Matin des magiciens*.
11. "Through the Gates of the Silver Key," in *Mountains of Madness*, 441. [This passage was conceived by Lovecraft's collaborator, E. Hoffmann Price—see his original sequel to "The Silver Key," entitled "The Lord of Illusion," first published

in *Crypt of Cthulhu* no. 10 (1982): 46–56—but the fact that Lovecraft retained the conception in the final draft may imply his relative agreement with its sentiments.]

4: The Horrific Bestiary

1. [Lovecraft to E. Toldridge, 8 Mar. 1929 (SL II.317).]
2. "It was the ultimate product of mammalian degeneration; the frightful outcome of isolated spawning, multiplication, and cannibal nutrition above and below the ground; the embodiment of all the snarling chaos and grinning fear that lurk behind life." See "The Lurking Fear," in *Dagon*, 199.
3. "The natives are now repellently decadent, having gone far along that path of retrogression so common in many New-England backwaters. They have come to form a race by themselves, with the well-defined mental and physical stigmata of degeneracy and inbreeding. The average of their intelligence is woefully low, whilst their annals reek of overt viciousness and of half-hidden murders, incests, and deeds of almost unnamable violence and perversity." See "The Dunwich Horror," in *Dunwich Horror*, 157.
4. *Dunwich Horror*, 174–75.
5. [Ibid., 177.]
6. "They were pinkish beings above five feet long; with crustaceous bodies bearing vast pairs of dorsal fins or membraneous wings and several sets of articulated limbs and with a sort of convoluted ellipsoid, covered with multitudes of very short antennae, where a head would ordinarily be." "The Whisperer in Darkness," in *Dunwich Horror*, 210.
7. [Actually, it is mentioned that Yuggoth (= Pluto) is only their "main *immediate* abode" and that "the main body of the beings inhabits strangely organised abysses wholly beyond the utmost reach of any human imagination." *Dunwich Horror*, 240.]
8. "Out of the fungus-ridden earth steamed up a vaporous corpse-light, yellow and diseased, which bubbled and lapped to a gigantic height in vague outlines half human and half monstrous, through which I could see the chimney and fireplace beyond. It was all eyes, wolfish and mocking, and the rugose insect-like head dissolved at the top to a thin stream of mist which curled putridly about and finally vanished up the chimney." "The Shunned House," in *Mountains of Madness*, 257.
9. "I cannot even hint what it was like, for it was a compound of all that is unclean, uncanny, unwelcome, abnormal, and detestable. It was the ghoulish shade of decay, antiquity, and desolation; the putrid, dripping eidolon of unwholesome revelation, the awful baring of that which the merciful earth should always hide. God knows it was not of this world—or no longer of this world—yet to my horror I saw in its eaten-away and bone-revealing outlines a leering, abhorrent travesty on the human shape; and in its mouldy, disintegrating apparel an unspeakable quality that chilled me even more." "The Outsider," in *Dunwich Horror*, 51.
10. [*Mountains of Madness*, 101.]
11. See Louis Vax, *La Séduction de l'étrange*, 22.

5: The Depths of Horror

1. [*Dagon*, 199.]
2. Bachelard, *La Poétique de l'espace*, 37.

3. Bachelard, *La Terre et les rêveries du repos,* 104.
4. [*Mountains of Madness,* 238.]
5. [*Dagon,* 277.]
6. Bachelard, *L'Air et les songes,* 122.
7. *Dagon,* 260.
8. [Ibid.]
9. [Ibid., 213.]
10. *Dunwich Horror,* 431.
11. [Lévy may have been making reference here to the French title of "The Shadow out of Time," "Dans L'Abîme du temps."]
12. [Poe's *Narrative of A. Gordon Pym* is often cited as a model or source for Lovecraft's work.]
13. *Mountains of Madness,* 105.
14. [*Dunwich Horror,* 228.]
15. "L'art de faire peur"; see the article of that name by Louis Vax.

6: The Horrors of Heredity

1. [*Dunwich Horror,* 14.]
2. Ibid., 20.
3. [Ibid., 305.]
4. [*Mountains of Madness,* 148.]
5. See *Dunwich Horror,* 14.
6. *The Dream-Quest of Unknown Kadath,* in *Mountains of Madness,* 338.
7. *Dagon,* 73.
8. [Lévy has compressed de la Poer's howls; for the entire text see *Dunwich Horror,* 45.]

7: Cthulhu

1. [*Dunwich Horror,* 226.]
2. [This is perhaps what Matthew H. Onderdonk was referring to when he noted that by Lovecraft's time "science fiction had already seen most of its best days. . . . This type of story in the past had always had a punch because it was so breathlessly futuristic. . . . Now, the products of research bid fair to outstrip the finest imaginings of our visionaries in literature. . . . The fictional prophets had been vindicated, of course, but unfortunately they stand in danger of being superseded by the news items in our daily papers!" "The Lord of R'lyeh" (1945), rpt. *Lovecraft Studies* 2, no. 2 (fall 1982): 12–13.]
3. Lovecraft himself reflected upon the problem in "Some Notes on Interplanetary Fiction" (*Marginalia,* 140–47). His remarks prove that he felt himself very far from authors of science fiction.
4. [Lovecraft to Farnsworth Wright, 5 July 1927 (SL II.150).]
5. *The Dream-Quest of Unknown Kadath,* in *Mountains of Madness,* 308.
6. [He also took on this form in his very first appearance in Lovecraft, in the prose-poem "Nyarlathotep" (1920).]
7. [Invented by Clark Ashton Smith.]
8. "The Dunwich Horror," in *Dunwich Horror,* 170.

9. ". . . men of a very low, mixed-blooded, and mentally aberrant type." See "The Call of Cthulhu," in *Dunwich Horror*, 139.

10. [Ibid., 136.]

11. "The Thing cannot be described—there is no language for such abysms of shrieking and immemorial lunacy, such eldritch contradictions of all matter, force, and cosmic order." Ibid., 152.

12. "Vast, Polyphemus-like, and loathsome, it darted like a stupendous monster of nightmare to the monolith, about which it flung its gigantic scaly arms, the while it bowed its hideous head and gave vent to certain measured sounds." See "Dagon," in *Dagon*, 18.

13. [Tsathoggua was invented by Clark Ashton Smith, but was readily incorporated by Lovecraft into his myth-cycle.]

14. [Ghatanothoa was created in Lovecraft's revision of Hazel Heald's "Out of the Eons."]

8: Unholy Cults

1. [*The Case of Charles Dexter Ward*, in *Mountains of Madness*, 205.]

2. [*The Cancer of Superstition*, cowritten with C. M. Eddy, Jr., was published in *Dark Brotherhood*, 246–61.]

3. Louis Vax, "Fantastique et croyance," in *La Séduction de l'étrange*, 163.

4. [Lovecraft said the same thing in "Supernatural Horror in Literature": "It may be well to remark here that occult believers are probably less effective than materialists in delineating the spectral and the fantastic, since to them the phantom world is so commonplace a reality that they tend to refer to it with less awe, remoteness, and impressiveness than do those who see in it an absolute and stupendous violation of the natural order" (*Dagon*, 417). See also Onderdonk, "The Lord of R'lyeh," for the same point.]

5. [The manuscript of this work is reproduced in facsimile in *Lovecraft at Last*, 104–5.]

6. See "The Making of a Hoax," in *Dark Brotherhood*, 262–67.

7. [It was invented by Clark Ashton Smith.]

8. [The book *is* cited directly—and not merely in the citation from the *Necronomicon* in the collaboration "Through the Gates of the Silver Key" (see *Mountains of Madness*, 430)—but Lovecraft's collaborator, E. Hoffmann Price, when preparing the typescript of the story, inadvertently left out the line containing the mention. For the correct text see now *Mountains of Madness*, 432.]

9. [Invented by Robert Bloch.]

10. [Invented by Robert E. Howard.]

11. [An actual work, of course. See now David E. Schultz's edition of the *Commonplace Book*, vol. 2: 43.]

12. [See *Mountains of Madness*, 151.]

13. ["The Horror at Red Hook," in *Dagon*, 247.]

14. [*Dagon*, 256. For Lovecraft's (not entirely accurate) explanation of this chant, see "The Incantation from Red Hook," in *The Occult Lovecraft*, 23–30.]

15. *Mountains of Madness*, 170.

16. [*Dunwich Horror*, 137.]

17. [Ibid., 196.]

18. [*Mountains of Madness*, 205.]

19. [*Dunwich Horror*, 160.]

20. Ibid., 196.

9: In the Chasms of Dream

1. [*Dunwich Horror*, 96.]
2. See Lovecraft to the Gallomo, 11 Dec. 1919 (SL I.94–97).
3. Lovecraft to R. Kleiner, 14 Dec. 192[0] (SL I.160–62). [The letter is misdated as 14 Dec. 1921 in SL.]
4. "*Celephaïs* . . . weaves together a large number of my recent dreams on a thread of pathos" (SL I.162).
5. Lovecraft to F. B. Long, 8 Feb. 1922 (SL I.166).
6. "I wonder, though, if I have a right to claim authorship of things I dream? I hate to take credit, when I did not really think out the picture with my own wits." Lovecraft to the Gallomo, 11 Dec. 1919 (SL I.97).
7. [These are the "night-gaunts" about whom he had been dreaming since he was six years old.]
8. [See Lovecraft to R. Kleiner, 21 May 1920 (SL I.114).]
9. [Ibid., 115. This dream, slightly metamorphosed, found its way into "The Call of Cthulhu."]
10. [This is the celebrated dream that Frank Belknap Long incorporated into his novel, *The Horror from the Hills* (1931). The dream is told, among other places, in Lovecraft to B. A. Dwyer, Nov. 1927 (SL II.188–97).]
11. See Lovecraft to D. Wandrei, 24 Nov. 1927 (SL II.200). [This dream was incorporated into "The Thing in the Moonlight," but David E. Schultz has now ascertained that that "fragment" is a compilation by J. Chapman Miske.]
12. See "Beyond the Wall of Sleep," in *Dagon*, 32.
13. "We live on memories—& I think that is all we can ever live on now, since mechanical invention has so appallingly divorced us from the soil & from those conditions of our forefathers around which the aesthetic feelings of the race are entwined." Lovecraft to C. A. Smith, 18 Feb. 1927 (SL II.104).
14. See "The Silver Key," in *Mountains of Madness*, 410.
15. Ibid., 410–11.
16. *L'Air et les songes.*
17. [*Mountains of Madness*, 332.]
18. [Ibid., 335.]
19. [This is the proper reading of the autograph manuscript, not "dholes."]
20. [Ibid., 337.]
21. [Ibid., 374.]
22. [Ibid., 406.]
23. [Ibid., 399.]
24. [Many of the conceptions in "Through the Gates of the Silver Key" were originated by Lovecraft's collaborator, E. Hoffmann Price; but, as noted earlier (see chap. 3, note 11), Lovecraft's retaining them in the final draft signals his approval of them.]
25. [*The Dream-Quest* was begun in late 1926 and finished on 22 Jan. 1927 (Derleth's assertion that it was written in the early 1920s and over the course of many years is entirely unfounded); during this time "The Silver Key" was written. E. Hoffmann Price sent Lovecraft his draft of "Through the Gates of the Silver Key" in Oct. 1932, but Lovecraft did not finish revising (i.e., rewriting) it until April 1933.]

10: From Fable to Myth

1. *Aspects du mythe*, 15.
2. [*Dunwich Horror*, 385.]

3. [If anything Lévy means the "Elder Gods," though their involvement with the Old Ones was in any case a fabrication of August Derleth's (see chap. 7).]

4. *L'Air et les songes*, 225.

5. See on this subject Louis Pauwels and Jacques Bergier, *Le Matin des magiciens*, part 2, chaps. 5 and 6.

6. Eliade, *Aspects du mythe*, 45.

Conclusion

1. See "Tales of the Marvellous and the Ridiculous," in *Classics and Commercials*, 286–90.

2. [Hawthorne is perhaps a likelier source for this; see Burleson, "H. P. Lovecraft: The Hawthorne Influence," passim.]

BIBLIOGRAPHY

Chronology of Lovecraft's Fiction

The Noble Eavesdropper (1897?) (nonextant)

The Little Glass Bottle (1897)

The Secret Cave or John Lees Adventure (1898)

The Mystery of the Grave-Yard (1898)

The Haunted House (1898/1902) (nonextant)

The Secret of the Grave (1898/1902) (nonextant)

John, the Detective (1898/1902) (nonextant)

The Mysterious Ship (1902)

The Beast in the Cave (21 April 1905)

The Picture (1907) (nonextant)

The Alchemist (1908)

The Tomb (June 1917)

Dagon (July 1917)

A Reminiscence of Dr. Samuel Johnson (1917)

Polaris (May? 1918)

The Mystery of Murdon Grange (1918) (nonextant)

The Green Meadow (with W. V. Jackson) (1918/19)

Beyond the Wall of Sleep (1919)

Memory (1919)

Old Bugs (1919)

The Transition of Juan Romero (16 Sept. 1919)

The White Ship (Nov. 1919)

The Doom That Came to Sarnath (3 Dec. 1919)

The Statement of Randolph Carter (Dec. 1919)

The Terrible Old Man (28 Jan. 1920)

The Tree (1920)

The Cats of Ulthar (15 June 1920)

The Temple (1920)

Facts concerning the Late Arthur Jermyn and His Family (1920)

The Street (1920?)

Life and Death (1920?) (lost)

Poetry and the Gods (with Anna Helen Crofts) (1920)

Celephaïs (early Nov. 1920)

From Beyond (16 Nov. 1920)

Nyarlathotep (early Dec. 1920)

The Picture in the House (12 Dec. 1920)

The Crawling Chaos (with W. V. Jackson) (1920/21)

Ex Oblivione (1920/21)

The Nameless City (Jan. 1921)

The Quest of Iranon (28 Feb. 1921)

The Moon-Bog (Mar. 1921)

The Outsider (1921)

The Other Gods (14 Aug. 1921)

The Music of Erich Zann (Dec. 1921)

Herbert West—Reanimator (Sept. 1921–mid 1922)

Hypnos (May 1922)

What the Moon Brings (5 June 1922)

Azathoth (June 1922)

The Horror at Martin's Beach (with Sonia Greene) (June 1922)

The Hound (Sept. 1922)

The Lurking Fear (Nov. 1922)

The Rats in the Walls (Aug./Sept. 1923)

The Unnamable (1923)

Ashes (with C. M. Eddy, Jr.) (1923)

The Ghost-Eater (with C. M. Eddy, Jr.) (1923)

The Loved Dead (with C. M. Eddy, Jr.) (1923)

The Festival (1923)

Deaf, Dumb, and Blind (with C. M. Eddy, Jr.) (1924?)

Under the Pyramids (with Harry Houdini) (Feb.–Mar. 1924)

The Shunned House (Oct. 1924)

The Horror at Red Hook (1–2 Aug. 1925)

He (11 Aug. 1925)

In the Vault (18 Sept. 1925)

The Descendant (1926?)

Cool Air (March 1926)

The Call of Cthulhu (summer 1926)

Two Black Bottles (with Wilfred B. Talman) (July–Oct. 1926)

Pickman's Model (1926)

The Silver Key (1926)

The Strange High House in the Mist (9 Nov. 1926)

The Dream-Quest of Unknown Kadath (autumn? 1926–22 Jan. 1927)

The Case of Charles Dexter Ward (Jan.–1 Mar. 1927)

The Colour out of Space (Mar. 1927)

The Very Old Folk (2 Nov. 1927)

The Last Test (with Adolphe de Castro) (1927)

History of the *Necronomicon* (1927)

The Curse of Yig (with Zealia Bishop) (1928)

Ibid (1928?)

The Dunwich Horror (summer 1928)

The Electric Executioner (with Adolphe de Castro) (1929?)

The Mound (with Zealia Bishop) (Dec. 1929–early 1930)

Medusa's Coil (with Zealia Bishop) (May 1930)

The Whisperer in Darkness (24 Feb.–26 Sept. 1930)

At the Mountains of Madness (Feb.–22 Mar. 1931)

The Shadow over Innsmouth (Nov.?–3 Dec. 1931)

The Trap (with Henry S. Whitehead) (1931)

The Dreams in the Witch House (Jan.–28 Feb. 1932)

The Man of Stone (with Hazel Heald) (1932)

The Horror in the Museum (with Hazel Heald) (Oct. 1932)

Through the Gates of the Silver Key (with E. Hoffmann Price) (Oct. 1932–Apr. 1933)

Winged Death (with Hazel Heald) (1933)

Out of the Eons (with Hazel Heald) (1933)

The Thing on the Doorstep (21–24 Aug. 1933)

The Horror in the Burying-Ground (with Hazel Heald) (1933/35)

The Book (late 1933?)

The Tree on the Hill (with Duane W. Rimel) (May 1934)

The Battle That Ended the Century (with R. H. Barlow) (June 1934)

The Shadow out of Time (Nov. 1934–Mar. 1935)

"Till A' the Seas" (with R. H. Barlow) (Jan. 1935)

Collapsing Cosmoses (with R. H. Barlow) (June 1935)

The Challenge from Beyond (with C. L. Moore, A. Merritt, Robert E. Howard, and Frank Belknap Long) (Aug. 1935)

The Diary of Alonzo Typer (with William Lumley) (Oct. 1935)

The Haunter of the Dark (Nov. 1935)

In the Walls of Eryx (with Kenneth Sterling) (Jan. 1936)

The Night Ocean (with R. H. Barlow) (autumn? 1936)

The Disinterment (with Duane W. Rimel) (1936?)

Primary Sources

In English

At the Mountains of Madness and Other Novels. Ed. S. T. Joshi. Sauk City, Wis.: Arkham House, 1985.

Beyond the Wall of Sleep. Sauk City, Wis.: Arkham House, 1943.

Commonplace Book. Ed. David E. Schultz. West Warwick, R.I.: Necronomicon Press, 1987. 2 vols.

Collected Poems. Sauk City, Wis.: Arkham House, 1963.

Dagon and Other Macabre Tales. Ed. S. T. Joshi. Sauk City, Wis.: Arkham House, 1986.

The Dark Brotherhood and Other Pieces. Sauk City, Wis.: Arkham House, 1966.

The Dunwich Horror and Others. Ed. S. T. Joshi. Sauk City, Wis.: Arkham House, 1984.

The Horror in the Museum and Other Revisions. Sauk City, Wis.: Arkham House, 1970.

In Defence of Dagon. Ed. S. T. Joshi. West Warwick, R.I.: Necronomicon Press, 1985.

Juvenilia: 1897–1905. Ed. S. T. Joshi. West Warwick, R.I.: Necronomicon Press, 1984.

Lovecraft at Last. By H. P. Lovecraft and Willis Conover. Arlington, Va.: Carrollton-Clark, 1975.

The Lovecraft Collectors Library. Ed. George Wetzel. North Tonawanda, N.Y.: SSR Publications, 1952–55. 7 vols. Rpt. in 1 vol. Madison, Wis.: Strange Co., 1979.

Marginalia. Sauk City, Wis.: Arkham House, 1944.

The Occult Lovecraft. With additional material by Anthony Raven. Saddle River, N.J.: Gerry de la Ree, 1975.

The Outsider and Others. Sauk City, Wis.: Arkham House, 1939.

Saturnalia and Other Poems. Ed. S. T. Joshi. Bloomfield, N.J.: Cryptic Publications, 1984.

Selected Letters: 1911–1937. Ed. August Derleth, Donald Wandrei, and James Turner. Sauk City, Wis.: Arkham House, 1965–76. 5 vols.

The Shuttered Room and Other Pieces. Sauk City, Wis.: Arkham House, 1959.

Some Notes on a Nonentity. Annotated by August Derleth. London: Arkham House/Villiers Publications, 1963.

Something about Cats and Other Pieces. Sauk City, Wis.: Arkham House, 1949.

Supernatural Horror in Literature. New York: Ben Abramson, 1945; New York: Dover Publications, 1973.

Uncollected Prose and Poetry. Ed. S. T. Joshi and Marc A. Michaud. West Warwick, R.I.: Necronomicon Press, 1978–82. 3 vols.

Writings in The United Amateur: *1915–1925.* Ed. Marc A. Michaud. West Warwick, R.I.: Necronomicon Press, 1976.

Translations into French

L'Affaire Charles Dexter Ward. Trans. Jacques Papy. Paris: J'ai Lu, 1972.

La Couleur tombée du ciel. Trans. Jacques Papy. Paris: Denoël, 1954.

Dagon et autres récits de terreur. Trans. Paule Pérez. Paris: Pierre Belfond, 1969; Paris: J'ai Lu, 1972.

Dans l'abime du temps. Trans. Jacques Papy. Paris: Denoël, 1954.

Démons et merveilles. Trans. Bernard Noël. Paris: Deux Rives, 1955; Paris: Union Générale d'Editions (10/18), 1963; Paris: Editions Opta/André Sauret, 1976.

Epouvante et surnaturel en littérature. Trans. Jacques Bergier and François Truchaud. Paris: Christian Bourgois, 1969. Trans. Bernard Da Costa. Paris: Christian Bourgois, 1971.

L'Horreur dans la musée: Les révisions de Lovecraft. Trans. Jacques Parsons. Paris: Christian Bourgois, 1975; Paris: France Loisirs, 1977 (2 vols.).

Je suis d'ailleurs. Trans. Yves Rivière. Paris: Denoël, 1961.

Lettres. Ed. Francis Lacassin. Trans. Jacques Parsons. Paris: Christian Bourgois, 1978. Vol. 1 only.

Night Ocean et autres nouvelles. Trans. Jean-Paul Mourlon. Paris: Pierre Belfond, 1986.

Par delà le mur du sommeil. Trans. Jacques Papy. Paris: Denoël, 1956.

Secondary Sources

Bachelard, Gaston. *L'Air et les songes.* Paris: Corti, 1943.

———. *La Poétique de l'espace.* Paris: P.U.F., 1957.

139

————. *La Terre et les rêveries du repos.* Paris: Corti, 1948.

Buhle, Paul. "Dystopia as Utopia: Howard Phillips Lovecraft and the Unknown Content of American Horror Literature." *Minnesota Review* no. 6 (spring 1976): 118–31. Rpt. in Joshi, *Four Decades of Criticism* (q.v.).

Burleson, Donald R. *H. P. Lovecraft: A Critical Study.* Westport, Conn.: Greenwood Press, 1983.

————. "H. P. Lovecraft: The Hawthorne Influence." *Extrapolation* 22, no. 3 (fall 1981): 262–69.

Cook, W. Paul. *In Memoriam: Howard Phillips Lovecraft—Recollections, Appreciations, Estimates.* North Montpelier, Vt.: Driftwind Press, 1941; West Warwick, R.I.: Necronomicon Press, 1977.

Davis, Sonia H. (Greene). *The Private Life of H. P. Lovecraft.* Ed. S. T. Joshi. West Warwick, R.I.: Necronomicon Press, 1985.

de Camp, L. Sprague. *Lovecraft: A Biography.* Garden City, N.Y.: Doubleday, 1975.

Derleth, August. *H. P. L.: A Memoir.* New York: Ben Abramson, 1945.

Eliade, Mircea. *Aspects du mythe.* Paris: Gallimard, 1963.

Everts, R. Alain. "Howard Phillips Lovecraft and Sex: Or the Sex Life of a Gentleman." *Nyctalops* 2, no. 2 (July 1974): 19.

Faig, Kenneth W. *H. P. Lovecraft: His Life, His Work.* West Warwick, R.I.: Necronomicon Press, 1979.

Joshi, S. T. "The Development of Lovecraftian Studies, 1971–82." *Lovecraft Studies* 3, no. 1 (spring 1984): 32–36; 3, no. 2 (fall 1984): 62–71; 4, no. 1 (spring 1985): 18–28; 4, no. 2 (fall 1985): 54–65.

———— (ed.) *H. P. Lovecraft: Four Decades of Criticism.* Athens, Ohio: Ohio University Press, 1980.

————. *H. P. Lovecraft and Lovecraft Criticism: An Annotated Bibliography.* Kent, Ohio: Kent State University Press, 1981.

————. *Reader's Guide to H. P. Lovecraft.* Mercer Island, Wash.: Starmont House, 1982.

Koki, Arthur S. "H. P. Lovecraft: An Introduction to His Life and Writings." M.A. thesis, Columbia University, 1962.

Leiber, Fritz. "A Literary Copernicus." In Lovecraft's *Something about Cats* (q.v.). In Joshi, *Four Decades of Criticism* (q.v.).

Lévy, Maurice. "Fascisme et fantastique, ou le cas Lovecraft." *Caliban* no. 7 (1970): 67–78.

Long, Frank Belknap. *Howard Phillips Lovecraft: Dreamer on the Nightside.* Sauk City, Wis.: Arkham House, 1975.

Mariconda, Steven J. "Notes on the Prose Realism of H. P. Lovecraft." *Lovecraft Studies* 4, no. 1 (spring 1985): 3–12.

Mosig, Dirk W. "H. P. Lovecraft: Myth-Maker." *The Miskatonic* 4, no. 1 (Feb. 1976): 12–18. In Joshi, *Four Decades of Criticism* (q.v.).

Murray, Will. "The Dunwich Chimera and Others: Correlating the Cthulhu Mythos." *Lovecraft Studies* 3, no. 1 (spring 1984): 10–24.

Onderdonk, Matthew H. "The Lord of R'lyeh." *Fantasy Commentator* 1, no. 6 (spring 1945): 103–14. *Lovecraft Studies* 2, no. 2 (fall 1982): 8–17.

Pauwels, Louis, and Jacques Bergier. *Le Matin des magiciens.* Paris: Gallimard, 1960. New York: Stein & Day, 1964; New York: Avon Books, 1968 (as *The Morning of the Magicians;* trans. Rollo Myers).

Price, Robert M. "Demythologizing Cthulhu." *Lovecraft Studies* 3, no. 1 (spring 1984): 3–9, 24.

———. "Higher Criticism and the *Necronomicon.*" *Lovecraft Studies* 2, no. 1 (spring 1982): 3–13.

Rabkin, Eric S. *The Fantastic in Literature.* Princeton: Princeton University Press, 1976.

Russ, Joanna. "On the Fascination of Horror Stories, Including Lovecraft's." *Science-Fiction Studies* 7, no. 3 (Nov. 1980): 350–52.

St. Armand, Barton L. *H. P. Lovecraft: New England Decadent.* Albuquerque, N.Mex.: Silver Scarab Press, 1979.

———. *The Roots of Horror in the Fiction of H. P. Lovecraft.* Elizabethtown, N.Y.: Dragon Press, 1977.

Schultz, David E. "Who Needs the 'Cthulhu Mythos'?" *Lovecraft Studies* 5, no. 2 (fall 1986): 43–53.

Todorov, Tzvetan. *Introduction à la littérature fantastique.* Paris: Editions du Seuil, 1970. Cleveland: Press of Case Western Reserve University, 1973; Ithaca, N.Y.: Cornell University Press, 1975 (as *The Fantastic: A Structural Approach to a Literary Genre;* trans. Richard Howard).

Vax, Louis, "L'Art de faire peur." *Critique* nos. 100–101 (1959): 915–42, 1026–48.

———. *La Séduction de l'étrange.* Paris: P.U.F., 1965.

Wandrei, Donald. "Lovecraft in Providence." In Lovecraft's *The Shuttered Room and Other Pieces* (q.v.).

Wilson, Edmund. "Tales of the Marvellous and the Ridiculous." In Wilson's *Classics and Commercials: A Literary Chronicle of the Forties.* New York: Farrar, Straus, 1950.

INDEX

A

Abbess, The (Ireland), 13, 124 n. 14
Addison, Joseph, 25, 26
"Alchemist, The," 20
Alhazred, Abdul, 59, 89
Amateur journalism, 20
Anderson, Poul, 81
Antaeus, 36
Arkham, Mass., 37, 51, 68, 74, 89, 91, 100
Asselineau, Roger, 9
Astounding Stories, 23
At the Mountains of Madness, 60, 69–70, 80, 111
Augustine, Saint, 74
Azathoth, 67, 81–83, 113

B

Bachelard, Gaston, 49, 64–65, 102, 114
"Beast in the Cave, The," 20

Bergier, Jacques, 12, 51, 124 n. 7, 128 n. 5, 133 n. 5
"Beyond the Wall of Sleep," 49–50
Bierce, Ambrose, 14–15, 33, 124 n. 16
Bloch, Robert, 81, 131 n. 9
Book of Eibon, 82, 89
Book of Thoth, 89
Book of Wonder, The (Dunsany), 33, 107
Bosch, Hieronymus, 55
Boston, Mass., 21, 28, 36–37, 39, 65–66, 76, 104, 106–7
Bradbury, Ray, 81
Brooklyn, N.Y., 23
Brown, Charles Brockden, 13, 124 n. 15
Brown University, 19, 41
Buchan, John, 33
Bulwer-Lytton, Edward, 92
Burleson, Donald R., 133 n. 2

C

Cabau, Jacques, 9
Cabell, James Branch, 26

Caillois, Roger, 71
"Call of Cthulhu, The," 41, 67, 83, 93–
    94, 128 n. 16, 131 n. 9, 132 n. 9
Cancer of Superstition (Lovecraft-Eddy),
    87–88, 131 n. 2
Carter, Randolph, 40–41, 50, 59, 76,
    99–107, 112–113
Case of Charles Dexter Ward, The, 40, 42,
    74–75, 82–83, 90–91, 94–95, 106,
    128 n. 10
"Cats of Ulthar, The," 125 n. 24
"Celephaïs," 98, 132 n. 4
Chambers, Robert W., 15, 124 n. 19
Christianity, 30–32, 92
Cole, Ira A., 20, 31
"Colour out of Space, The," 37, 70, 74,
    127 n. 5
Concord, Mass., 104
Conservative, The, 26
"Cool Air," 25
Crawford, Francis Marion, 15, 33,
    124 n. 18
Cthulhu, 18, 41, 67, 83, 89, 92, 112–13
Cthulhu Mythos, 12–13, 79–85, 88, 101,
    104–5, 109–15, 117–20. *See also*
    Lovecraft Mythos
Cultes des Goules (d'Erlette), 89

D

Daemonolatreia (Remigius), 90
Dagon, 40–41, 83, 113
"Dagon," 20, 84, 128 n. 13, 131 n. 12
"Damned Thing, The" (Bierce), 14
Darwin, Charles, 30
Davis, Sonia H., 22, 27, 126 n. 44
de Camp, L. Sprague, 123 n. 3, 126 n.
    44
de la Mare, Walter, 52
De Masticatione Mortuorum (Rohr), 90
"Dead Smile, The" (Crawford), 15
"Death of Halpin Frayser, The"
    (Bierce), 14
Democritus, 30
Derleth, August, 8–9, 11, 24, 81, 89,
    124 n. 6, 133 n. 3
Deutsch, Michel, 12
Devil's Dictionary, The (Bierce), 14,
    124 n. 16
Doré, Gustave, 47
Dream-Quest of Unknown Kadath, The,
    41, 59, 76, 81–82, 100–107, 117,
    125 n. 24, 128 n. 15, 132 n. 25

Dreams, 46–52, 69, 97–108, 114, 118–19
"Dreams in the Witch House, The," 39,
    49–51, 64, 93, 99, 128 n. 8
Dunsany, Lord, 32–33, 36, 38, 49–50,
    64, 81, 84–85, 107
Dunwich, Mass., 37, 82
"Dunwich Horror, The," 57–60, 82–83,
    94–96, 105–6, 129 n. 3

E

Eddy, C. M., Jr., 131 n. 2
Edgar Huntly (Brown), 13, 124 n. 15
Einstein, Albert, 51–53, 88, 128 n. 9
Eliade, Mircea, 110–11, 115
England, 15, 18, 25–27, 66, 77, 125 n. 2
Epicurus, 30
Ernoult, Claude, 12
Esprit, 12
Everts, R. Alain, 125 n. 16

F

"Facts concerning the Late Arthur Jer-
    myn and His Family," 77
"Fall of the House of Usher, The"
    (Poe), 13, 32, 77
Fantastic, the, 11–14, 33–37, 42, 45–46,
    50–51, 71, 78, 95, 107, 118–20;
    American, 13–16
"Festival, The," 47, 66, 75, 90, 93
Fiske, John, 88, 114
"For the Blood Is the Life" (Crawford),
    15
Frazer, James George, 88, 114
"From Beyond," 59

G

Galpin, Alfred, 20, 27
Gamwell, Annie E. P., 28
George, Daniel, 117
Ghatanothoa, 84, 131 n. 14
Gods of Pegāna, The (Dunsany), 33, 84
Godwin, William, 92
Golden Dawn, Order of the, 51
Gothic novel, 13, 15, 33, 52, 92, 99, 119
Graeco-Roman mythology, 19, 84–85,
    113–14
Greene, Sonia H. *See* Davis, Sonia H.
Grimm brothers, 19

H

"Haunter of the Dark, The," 64, 82, 97, 105
Hawthorne, Nathaniel, 14–15, 19, 133 n. 2
"He," 23, 42, 46, 48, 128 n. 2, 128 n. 3
Heald, Hazel, 131 n. 14
"Herbert West—Reanimator," 21, 40, 62, 128 n. 11
Herne, Cahier de L', 12, 124 n. 10
Hill of Dreams, The (Machen), 33
Hitler, Adolf, 27, 126 n. 44
Hoffmann, E. T. A., 33
Home Brew, 23, 125 n. 18
"Horror at Red Hook, The," 23, 65–68, 91, 93–94, 131 n. 14
Houdini, Harry, 87
"Hound, The," 21, 40, 128 n. 12
Howard, Robert E., 81, 131 n. 10
Huxley, Thomas Henry, 30
"Hypnos," 50, 98, 124 n. 7, 128 n. 7

I

Image du Monde (Gautier de Metz), 90
Innsmouth, Mass., 37
Ireland, William Henry, 13

J

James, Henry, 15, 124 n. 17
James, M. R., 33
Jefferson, Thomas, 13
Joyce, James, 26
Jurgen (Cabell), 26

K

King in Yellow, The (Chambers), 15
Kingsport, Mass., 47, 64, 66, 75
Kleiner, Rheinhart, 20, 22, 25, 28, 31
Ku Klux Klan, 27

L

Lathom, Francis, 13
LeFanu, J. Sheridan, 52
Leucippus, 30
Lewis, Matthew Gregory, 13, 52
Liber Damnatus, 90
Long, Frank Belknap, 9, 20, 22–24, 26, 28, 81, 132 n. 10

Lovecraft, H. P., ancestry, 18; appearance, 24–25; childhood, 18–20, 78; correspondence, 17, 20–21, 24, 39, 115, 119, 128 n. 5; dreams, 32, 52, 97–99, 114, 132 n. 9, 10; health, 18–20, 78; literary influences, 32–33, 119; literary theory, 33–34; marriage, 22–23; philosophy, 30–32, 51, 56, 114–15, 119–20, 131 n. 4; political and racial views, 26–30, 46, 48, 61–62, 66, 114–15; religious views, 30–31, 87–88; sexuality, 22, 25–26, 60, 108; travels, 21, 24
Lovecraft, Sarah Susan (mother), 19, 21
Lovecraft, Winfield Scott (father), 18–19
Lovecraft Mythos, 123 n. 5. *See also* Cthulhu Mythos
Loveman, Samuel, 30, 98
Lucretius, 30
"Lurking Fear, The," 38, 57, 61, 63, 67, 74, 125 n. 18, 127 n. 6, 129 n. 2

M

Machen, Arthur, 18, 33, 51, 119
Marblehead, Mass., 21, 36–37, 39
Marvel Tales, 23
Matin des magiciens, Le (Pauwels-Bergier), 12
Maturin, Charles Robert, 52, 92
Mein Kampf (Hitler), 27, 126 n. 44
"Metzengerstein" (Poe), 13
"Middle Toe of the Right Foot, The" (Bierce), 14
Miskatonic University, 41, 51, 68, 89, 96
Miske, J. Chapman, 132 n. 11
Moe, Maurice W., 20, 30–31
Morton, James F., 20, 22, 27
Mosig, Dirk W., 8
Munn, H. Warner, 124 n. 9
"Music of Erich Zann, The," 47–48
Myth, 81–85, 88, 102, 108–15, 118–20

N

Necronomicon (Alhazred), 59, 82, 84, 88–89, 91–92, 96, 101, 105
New England, 16, 18, 21, 23–24, 27, 35–43, 48, 56, 73, 98, 119, 127 n. 4
New York City, 19, 22, 24, 28, 30, 36, 46–48, 61, 65–66, 91, 93, 127 n. 3
Newport, R.I., 36–37, 104

Nietzsche, Friedrich, 30
Nyarlathotep, 18, 64–65, 82–83, 101, 103–5, 113
"Nyarlathotep," 98, 130 n. 6

O

Occultism, 51–52
Onderdonk, Matthew H., 130 n. 2, 131 n. 4
Orton, Vrest, 124 n. 9
"Out of the Eons," 131 n. 14
"Outsider, The," 21, 25, 61, 108, 129 n. 9

P

Paris, 47
Pauwels, Louis, 12, 51, 133 n. 5
Phillips, Whipple Van Buren (Lovecraft's grandfather), 18
"Pickman's Model," 65, 73, 76, 104
Piranesi, G. B., 45
Planète, 12, 124 n. 7
Pnakotic Manuscripts, 89
Poe, Edgar Allan, 13–15, 19, 32–33, 38–39, 47, 69, 77, 117–18, 127 n. 71, 127 n. 72, 130 n. 12
"Polaris," 20
Pompeii, 18
Portsmouth, N.H., 21, 37
Price, E. Hoffmann, 128 n. 11, 131 n. 8, 132 n. 25
Price, Robert M., 8
Providence, R.I., 17–19, 22–24, 26, 28, 32–33, 36–37, 39, 42, 64, 82, 104, 107, 113
"Purloined Letter, The" (Poe), 13

Q

Quebec, 24

R

Radcliffe, Ann, 13, 15
"Rats in the Walls, The," 66–68, 77–78, 125 n. 24
Ray, Jean, 46, 92
Rhode Island Journal of Astronomy, The, 19
Richmond, Va., 24
Rieux, Madame de, 124 n. 13

R'lyeh, 41
Roche, Regina Maria, 13
Rosa, Salvator, 37, 127 n. 5
"Ruelle tenebreuse, La" (Ray), 46

S

Saducismus Triumphatus (Glanvil), 90
Salem, Mass., 14, 16, 21, 36–37, 76, 104, 107, 127 n. 4
Schopenhauer, Arthur, 30
Schultz, David E., 8, 131 n. 11, 132 n. 11
Science fiction, 70, 76, 79–80, 130 n. 2
Seignolles, 92
Seven Cryptical Books of Hsan, 89, 101
"Shadow out of Time, The," 68–69, 99, 110–11, 130 n. 11
"Shadow over Innsmouth, The," 56–57, 67, 74–76, 83–84, 99, 105–6
Shelley, Percy Bysshe, 92
Shub-Niggurath, 84
"Shunned House, The," 39, 59, 64, 67, 129 n. 8
"Silver Key, The," 99–100, 106, 112, 132 n. 25
Sime, S. H., 33, 49, 107
Smith, Clark Ashton, 20, 24, 81, 130 n. 7, 131 n. 7 (ch. 8), 131 n. 13 (ch. 7)
"Statement of Randolph Carter, The," 40, 97–98
"Strange High House in the Mist, The," 38, 64, 127 n. 7
"Suitable Surroundings, The" (Bierce), 14–15
"Supernatural Horror in Literature," 33, 127 n. 75, 131 n. 4
Sword of Welleran, The (Dunsany), 33

T

"Temple, The," 128 n. 14
"Thing in the Moonlight, The," 132 n. 11
"Thing on the Doorstep, The," 42, 91
"Through the Gates of the Silver Key," 45, 52–53, 105–6, 113, 128 n. 11, 131 n. 8, 132 n. 24, 25
Tierney, Richard L., 8
"Tomb, The," 20, 75
Tsathoggua, 84, 131 n. 13
Turn of the Screw, The (James), 15
Tuzet, Hélène, 9
Tyler, Royal, 124 n. 12

U

Ulysses (Joyce), 26
'Umr at-Tawil, 84, 106
Unaussprechlichen Kulten (von Juntz), 89
United Amateur Press Association, 20–22, 125 n. 14

V

Vax, Louis, 74, 88, 130 n. 15

W

Wandrei, Donald, 24, 124 n. 6
Weird Tales, 23

"Whisperer in Darkness, The," 59, 70, 79, 83, 128 n. 6, 7
"White Ship, The," 20
Wilkins-Freeman, Mary E., 15, 124 n. 20
Wilson, Edmund, 117
Wind in the Rose-Bush, The (Wilkins-Freeman), 15

Y

Yog-Sothoth, 18, 24, 57, 61, 82–84, 88–89, 91–92, 95–96, 106, 113
Yuggoth, 59, 70, 129 n. 7

Maurice Lévy is a respected French critic and editor, author of *Le Roman "gothique" anglais, Images du roman noir*, and *Roman et société en Angleterre au XVIII-siècle* (with Jean Ducrocq and Suzy Halimi). He teaches at the University of Toulouse.

S. T. Joshi has written extensively on Lovecraft. In addition to many articles, he has published *H. P. Lovecraft: Four Decades of Criticism, H. P. Lovecraft and Lovecraft Criticism: An Annotated Bibliography, Reader's Guide to H. P. Lovecraft,* and a three-volume revised edition of Lovecraft's collected fiction. Mr. Joshi is the editor of *Lovecraft Studies* and *Studies in Weird Fiction.*

The manuscript was prepared for publication by Tom Seller. The art was drawn by Jason C. Eckhardt. The typeface for the text is Palatino. The display types are Albertus and Palatino. The cloth edition is printed on 55-lb. Glatfelter text paper and is bound in Holliston Mills' Roxite Linen.

Manufactured in the United States of America.